The Blindness of Odile

Pamella Bowen

GREEN AND PURPLE
PUBLISHING

The Blindness of Odile

ISBN 978-1-950190-09-6

Green and Purple Publishing
California, USA
www.greenandpurplepublishing.com

This is a work of fiction. Characters and names are invented and should not be taken to refer to actual persons, living or dead.

Formatting by Therese Kay Creative

NOTES TO THE READER

SAINT ODILE

Legend tells that Odile of Alsace was born blind in about 662 CE but gained her sight after a kindly bishop baptized her. Her miracles included splitting a mountain and saving her brother's life.

Source: https://en.wikipedia.org/wiki/Odile_of_Alsace

SAYING HER NAME

It will help if you pronounce the main character's name "Oh-DEEL."

DEDICATION

This book is dedicated to all my traveling companions who explored the UK with me, beginning in 1970, with Kathie Carpenter.

BOOKS MENTIONED IN THE TEXT, all still in print and available:

The Interior Castle by Teresa of Avila

The Practice of the Presence of God by Brother Lawrence

The Cloud of Unknowing by Anonymous

BIBLE QUOTATIONS are from the New Revised Standard Version, first published in 1989, though that is an anachronism in a 1970 story.

1

Sophisticated

O dile Travers knew her seat was in row 35 of the Boeing 707, so she kept her eyes on the little numbers as she made her way down the aisle of the plane. She had never been on a jet plane before, had no idea what she was doing, and wanted to look cool, sophisticated, and cosmopolitan. When she reached row 35, people were already seated in two of the three seats. She stared at them, not knowing what to say.

"Oh, I bet you are our seat mate," the paunchy man in the aisle seat said.

His wife chimed in, "Would you like the window seat, dear?"

"Yes, that will be fine," Odile said. The couple vacated their seats so she could squeeze into the window seat, putting her tote-bag next to her feet. Though the man offered to stow it in the overhead compartment with her raincoat, she said no. She wanted to have the bag with her in case she

1

needed something from it, like Kleenex, gum, or her book. She slipped off her low-heeled pumps that hurt her feet. She hadn't realized how far you had to walk in airports. Perhaps she should have worn her Keds, but they didn't really go with her polyester knit A-line dress. She had read about the proper thing to wear on airplanes in some magazines, and they said knits were just the thing, preferably in dark colors, that you could dress up with a change of accessories, maybe a scarf or a long necklace.

"Well, since we will be together for the next thirteen hours, we should introduce ourselves," the woman said. "I am Edna, and this is my husband Bill."

"I am Odile."

"Now that's an interesting name. And why are you flying to London, Odile?"

"I am starting my post-graduate work at Cambridge University, in international relations. I hope to work for the foreign service or at the UN. My bachelor's degree is in modern languages."

"Well, that is marvelous. Where did you earn your degree?"

"At Progress State College, here in California. My parents live in Progress, so it was an obvious choice."

"You didn't want to go away to school?"

"Oh, no. The thought of living in the dorm with a messy roommate put me off. I preferred to commute from home, keep things comfortable. I graduated in 1968. I have been working for the last two years as an assistant editor at the *Bulletin* newspaper, saving up money for my study abroad."

"Well, that is very ambitious of you. Editing seems like a challenging job."

"Not really. I am a perfectionist at heart, so I'm good at correcting other people's work. I catch those errors that others overlook," Odile said, smiling modestly, she hoped.

"And are you leaving a boyfriend at home when you are off studying in England?"

"Oh, no. Never seemed to find a guy up to my standards."

"Really? Perfectionism again?"

"Not really. I dated some during college, but there never seemed to be any chemistry. I am not attracted to men with red hair, in particular. Tall, dark, handsome, intelligent---those are my criteria." Odile glanced across to make sure Bill wasn't a redhead. He wasn't. "And I'm not much of a party girl because I don't drink. Never want to lose control of myself, I guess. Usually I drive myself on dates, meeting the guy there. That way if I get fed up, I can just go home. I don't have to depend on him. I like it that way."

"And what college will you be attending at Cambridge?"

"Well, that's a sore subject with me. I will be attending Newnham College, a women's school. I can only attend lectures in the men's colleges by enrolling in one of the women's colleges. England is far behind us in accepting women as equals. It irritates me that my diploma will say Newnham, not one of the more prestigious colleges."

"What makes you want to enter the foreign service?"

"I believe it's my destiny to do something great with my life. I was identified as gifted early on and graduated *magna cum laude.* I have always shown great facility with languages. I am fluent in Spanish, French, Italian, and Russian. Therefore, I have set my sights high."

"Do you feel you have a calling from God?"

Odile scoffed. "No. I don't believe in God. My parents stopped attending church, and I never felt the lack of it. Some people need something supernatural to make them feel safe. I don't. I am the captain of my own ship."

"There are many beautiful cathedrals and ecclesiastical buildings in England. You should visit them, even if you aren't a believer."

"Yes, I am fascinated by architecture and art. I can enjoy a visit to a church or a Greek temple whether I believe or not. They are some of man's greatest achievements."

3

"Have you been abroad before?"

"Oh, no. This is my first flight anywhere."

"Wonderful! I am glad we gave you the window seat. Now, if you need to get out to use the toilet, don't hesitate to ask us. We will gladly let you out."

"Thank you. I hope that won't be necessary."

Edna looked at Odile curiously. But indeed, Odile didn't ask to be let out to visit the toilet on the first leg of the flight, from Los Angeles to Ottawa. In Ottawa airport she used the WC, but again she held it from Ottawa to Gatwick airport. She didn't want to admit that she didn't know where the toilet was on the plane. Sophisticated world travelers knew all about planes and didn't have to ask.

———————— • ——————

Sophisticated world travelers also carried little fold-up umbrellas in their tote-bags in case of rain. But one can't carry an umbrella when one is burdened with a purse, a tote, and a suitcase, so when Odile emerged from Victoria station after taking the train from Gatwick, the pelting rain soaked her short hair, legs, and feet as she walked to her cheap hotel, several blocks away. She didn't know how to take a taxi, but she did have a map (now soggy) and thought the hotel looked near enough to walk to. When she approached hotel reception, she resembled a bedraggled waif, not a sophisticated world traveler.

"Your room is on the fourth floor, Miss," the desk clerk said. "The stairs are over there."

"There's no elevator?"

"Sorry. No lift, just the stairs."

There also was no porter in evidence. Odile wouldn't have wanted a porter because she didn't know how to tip one. In her soggy pumps, lugging all her bags, she climbed five flights of stairs. She expected it to be four flights, not knowing that the ground floor doesn't count in England. Her room was on what she would call the fifth floor, and her window looked out on the grimy brick wall of the adjacent building. She dropped her bags inside the small room, after fiddling with the skeleton key in the ancient door lock, and went to find the WC down the hall. When she sat down on the black seat of the old-fashioned pull-chain toilet, she found that she could not pee. Nothing came. She had clamped her distended bladder shut for too long. What would she do? What if she died on her first day in England and was found lying on the tiny hexagonal tiles with a burst bladder? She massaged her belly and breathed "god help me" unconsciously. Still nothing. After about a minute, tears started to leak from her eyes, and a little pee tinkled in the pot. Then more. Eventually, bladder empty, she wiped herself with the stiff, waxy toilet paper, pulled up her pantyhose, and went to her room, where she stripped off her wet dress, hose, and underwear. Kicking off the soaked, killing heels, she opened her case, put on her nightgown and crawled under the covers of the creaky, single bed. Odile really hated being wet. She also hated being out of familiar surroundings. Pulling the blanket over her head, she blocked out the sight of the shabby room and tried to sleep. Never mind that it was 11 o'clock in the morning.

———————— • • ————————

English money, food, and some better shoes topped Odile's list when she emerged next day onto the gray pavement. The rain had stopped, but the clouds lingered over the still-wet streets. She buttoned up her rain coat and set off in the direction of Barclay's Bank. There she signed over several of her American Express travellers cheques and received an assortment of odd-sized bills and some very heavy coins. She had studied the money in a copy of *England on $10 a Day* before she left home, but holding the real thing in her hand made her forget what she learned. She placed the sterling notes into her American wallet and realized they didn't fit. Trying to look confident as she walked out of the bank, she turned to her right and found a tea room with a sandwich board in front saying "Morning Coffee." A waitress came to her at a small corner table, and she ordered a ham sandwich and coffee.

"Black or white?" the waitress asked.

Not knowing what in the world white coffee might be, Odile said, "Black," even though she hated black coffee. At least there was a big bowl of sugar cubes on the table.

"Salt or mustard on the sandwich?"

"Mustard." She thought it odd to choose between salt and mustard, but when the sandwich came, she could barely eat it: the mustard was so sharp. She should have said salt. Luckily, the waitress brought her the bill on a saucer so she had time to sort through her money and find the appropriate note to cover the amount without looking too foolish. Odile was trying to navigate the mine field of a strange land with sophistication and aplomb. It was exhausting.

Next, she set off for the Clark's shoe shop the hotel desk clerk had suggested as a place for comfy walking shoes. Today, Odile wore her white Keds with bell-bottomed jeans and a knitted top. The heels were in the trash can in her hotel room.

The Clark's salesgirl said, "What can I find for you, Miss?"

"I need some comfortable walking shoes for exploring London. I wear a nine."

The clerk peered skeptically at Odile's feet.

"Let me just measure your feet. You don't look like a nine." Odile huffed to herself at the audacity of the salesgirl. But sure enough, on the Clark's measuring gauge, she wore a six-and-a-half. She bought a sturdy pair of brown lace-up oxfords, paid with the strange money, and walked toward the hotel, carrying the new shoes in a paper sack.

The street smelled of diesel exhaust and urine. Trucks splashed by in the gutter where limp cabbage leaves and other garbage stewed in the black mud. The same gritty dust that blew in the air coated the surfaces of the buildings, painting them sooty black. Odile looked into the shop windows she passed. The pastries in the bakery looked delicious, the greengrocer's fruits and vegetables were stacked colorfully, and the tobacconist's displayed ribboned boxes of chocolates. She was about to exult over the quaintness of English ways when she looked in at the butcher's. Dead rabbits, chickens, and pheasants hung from their necks in the window. Odile felt faint. What infernal place had she come to? Everything was wrong, backward, upside down here. In turning away from the butcher's window, she stepped awkwardly off the curb, slipped in the slimy gutter, and fell on her knees, letting go of her package which flew into the street.

"Here, Dearie, let me help you up," a crone with missing teeth said, lifting Odile by the elbow. "Are you all right?" The woman's breath stank.

"Yes, fine thank you. I just missed my footing," Odile said, trying to control her emotions. Her Keds were black with mud and her jeans soaked. The old woman handed her the new shoes, still in their bag. "I must get home," and Odile fled the scene before anyone could see her tears.

For the next few days, she explored dark, disorienting London, learning how to 'spend a penny' and ride the tube from one historical site to the next. Now that she knew her shoe size, she bought replacements for the ruined Keds at Marks and Spencer. She also bought two twinsets. England was a lot colder than California, and wearing a sweater over another sweater seemed a practical solution. She had to learn to call the outer sweater a 'cardy,' though. She was feeling a little more in control of her new life by the time she had to pack for Cambridge. She knew that Liverpool Street was the station she needed, and she knew her nearest tube stop was Sloane Square. Knowledge was power, and she was gaining knowledge every minute.

At Liverpool Street station, she asked the ticket seller for a one-way ticket to Cambridge. He corrected her when he handed her the ticket and her change, "Single to Cambridge." Then he gestured toward the platforms and said something incomprehensible. She supposed he was telling her what platform she needed, but she didn't catch it. She didn't want to admit she didn't understand him; that would not look cosmopolitan. She might be fluent in French and Russian, but she was struggling with English. Instead of asking him to repeat his directions, she stood among the crowd of travelers and stared up at the departure board overhead. So many trains, destinations, times, and platforms. Over a loudspeaker she heard a ringing tone followed by a woman's voice announcing trains arriving and departing. Odile could catch only a few of the words, spoken in a posh English accent, distorted by the amplification. The white figures on the black board began to swim as tears filled her eyes. She said to herself, "Come on, Odile. You are a smart cookie. You can figure this out." Taking a deep breath, she concentrated on the board, found Cambridge as a destination, noted the platform number and the departure time. Checking her watch, she saw that she had half an hour to wait. She would visit the WC. She had no idea how to find or use a train toilet, so she would go now in the station.

The large, tiled women's toilet smelled of urine and disinfectant. She fished one of the big, brown pennies out of her purse and put it into the slot in the door handle, which she turned and admitted herself to a large stall. Thank goodness it was so large, since she had dragged all her luggage into the WC with her, not having a companion to leave it with and not knowing about the 'left luggage' office. As she sat on the toilet, she read the notices in the stall. 'Beware of thieves,' 'Dispose of sanitary towels in the incinerator,' and 'Medicated' printed on the waxed toilet paper roll. She had seen 'City of Westminster' and 'Borough of London' printed on other toilet paper in public facilities. What could 'medicated' mean, and how did it affect your body when you wiped? She guessed that the printing and the horrible waxed surface were designed to deter anyone who would take a roll or two home with them. She was sure it worked.

When she left the stall, she looked around for the 'incinerator' as she washed her hands and dried them on the soggy roller towel. Sure enough, there on the wall was a white enameled appliance. 'Sanitary Towel Disposal' it said. A smudge of brown scorch ran up the wall above the contraption, from the smoke of burning blood and cotton. Odile was appalled and fascinated. Medicated toilet paper, incinerated feminine pads, and soggy communal roller towels. Baffling. Odile congratulated herself that she would not be buying or disposing of sanitary towels at all while she was here. At least she could avoid that land mine.

2

Cambridge

Odile held her breath for the first few days at Cambridge, controlling her emotions of dismay and confusion as best she could. Her room at Newnham was small and dingy, no better than the hotel in London, except her window had a view of slate roof tiles with a patch of blue sky above. She only had to climb three flights of stairs and push past two fire safety doors. The WC and bathrooms were down the hall, but she had a sink in her room where she could brush her teeth, wash up, and hand-wash her pantyhose and such. Putting a washstand in the room was the first English quirk she approved of; it enabled her to keep her privacy.

She was one of only two women in the lecture hall at Trinity one day. She made eye contact with a long-haired girl in a mini-skirt across the room. The girl smiled, picked up her books, and came across to sit by Odile.

"My name is Naomi. Naomi Warden," the girl said, offering her hand.

"I am Odile Travers," Odile said, shaking hands.

"Oh, you're an American! I've always wanted to go to America. Where in America are you from?"

"California."

"Brilliant! Welcome to Cambridge, Odile. Let's go have a drink when this is over, all right?"

"Sure. I'd like that." Odile busied herself with her notebook and pen. She didn't want Naomi to notice her discomposure. The girl's kindness had pierced Odile's armor of bravado, and tears threatened. Though most of the people she had met in England were polite and helpful, Naomi was the first to offer warmth.

"Let's go to the Town and Gown," Naomi said as they left Trinity. "It's across the green by the river."

"Why is it called that?"

"Oh, you know, there's always been tension between the town and the university, going way back to the middle ages. The owners of the place decided to acknowledge it by naming the pub Town and Gown, and they work to keep a convivial atmosphere, welcoming academics and locals. It's a good place to meet real people. Some of the gowny pubs are so snobbish. I'm sort of on the fence between town and gown, being a student but living at home here in Cambridge with my mum. What's your favorite drink, Odile?"

"I'll just have a Coke." Odile realized that a Coke wasn't very sophisticated, but she was still on her guard. She couldn't risk losing her cool, becoming too loquacious among strangers.

"All right." Naomi stepped up to the bar and asked the barman for a half of Strongbow, a Coke, and two packets of crisps. "Odile, do you want onion or salt and vinegar?"

"Which is better?"

"We'll have one of each," Naomi said.

"I notice you're an American. Do you want ice in that Coke?" the barman asked.

Odile was stunned to be addressed by the barman, a red-haired man with horn-rimmed glasses that slid down his freckled nose. "Yes, please," she said. Wouldn't you know it. The first man to speak to her had to be a redhead with glasses.

Naomi paid for the drinks, and the two women went to sit at a picnic table in the garden. The English all seemed addicted to cigarettes, and the Town and Gown was dense with smoke.

Odile liked both the onion and the vinegar crisps, which she would have called chips. The vinegar burned her tongue, but the taste was pleasant.

"What is Strongbow?" Odile asked.

"Cider. Here, have a taste," Naomi said, handing her the glass. It was sweet and fizzy, very drinkable, Odile thought.

"Mmm. That's good. I'll have one of those the next round." Just then, the barman, who must have been keeping an eye on the level in the women's glasses, appeared at the table with a tray in his hand.

"Ready for another?" he asked, smiling at both of them.

"Yes," Odile said, "two halves of Strongbow this time, and two more packets of crisps. And could you bring some napkins?"

The barman and Naomi both smiled.

"Yes, I'll bring some serviettes. Back in a tick."

"Oops. Blew it again," Odile said, feeling crushed. "What did I say this time?"

"I think you call them diapers, for babies," Naomi volunteered. "Complex language, English."

"I am so off-balance here. I'm trying so hard not to mess up."

"Maybe you need to relax, have some cider, and just be American. Most of us love Americans, you know. We forgive you all your barmy expressions."

"Thanks." Odile liked Naomi. Maybe she could relax a little, as long as she didn't lose sight of her ambitious goals.

When the barman returned with the order, he lingered.

"I've seen you in here a few times, haven't I?" he said to Naomi. "My name is Stewart."

"I'm Naomi," she said, offering her hand. "And this is my friend Odile." Odile shook his warm, soft hand.

"A pleasure to meet you both. Just let me know if I can bring you anything. Maybe some food. Fish and chips is the special today." And Stewart left, pushing his glasses up on his nose.

After fish and chips and three halves of Strongbow, Odile was relaxed enough to laugh, and look around the pub's garden at the other customers, especially the men. She smiled and flirted with the best looking ones, feeling their interest in her. Was it her accent or her attractiveness? When she and Naomi paid their bill, she even flirted with Stewart a little, giving him her warmest smile.

"Hope to see you ladies again soon," he said as they headed for the door.

Odile smiled over her shoulder and gave him a twiddle of her fingers in farewell. She staggered when she walked across the green toward Newnham. Cider was much stronger than Coke.

One Sunday Odile had to turn down Naomi's invitation for lunch at her mum's house because one of the dons from Christ's was hosting a garden party for the British ambassador to France. It was right up Odile's alley, and she couldn't miss the opportunity to make some connections in the foreign policy realm. As she walked through town to the professor's house, she passed under the arches of a stone cloister and heard peeping birds above her head. She stopped and looked up to see a row of baby swallow beaks peeking out of the mud nest, waiting for their mother bird to bring them dinner. Her heart stirred with love for the tiny creatures, and she yearned to stay, watching for the return of the mother. The voice of her ambition, however, spoke in her head, telling her not to be late for the garden party. She couldn't miss a chance that might give her career a boost.

At the party she took a glass of Pimm's punch, delicious and drinkable, and she feared stronger than it tasted, and tried to break into the conversation. No one seemed interested in what she had to say. No one seemed to care that she was American. No one seemed to care that she had graduated *magna cum laude*. She was coming to suspect that her education at a state college, no matter the honors, didn't prepare her to compete with the brightest and best at Cambridge. Why hadn't she gone to a high-power school? She set down her glass and slunk away from the garden without meeting the ambassador. She should have gone to lunch at Naomi's. She should have stayed to watch for the mother bird. When she passed under the cloister again, she looked and listened for the chicks, but they were hidden and silent.

She couldn't face her drab room at Newnham, so she sat on a bench by the river and stared at King's College chapel. Everything suddenly seemed so empty and meaningless. Whose fault was that? Who could she blame? Progress state? Her parents? The English? Cambridge? Another possibility pushed against her locked heart, trying to rear its ugly head, but she wouldn't allow it. The chapel glowed golden in the afternoon sun.

"I need a half of Strongbow," she said, and turned toward the Town and Gown. Stewart served her the cider and looked happy to see her.

"Say, Odile, my shift ends in about an hour. Could I take you for a meal?"

"Sure, I'll wait for you in the garden."

"Do you have Naomi's number? We could ask her, too," he said, pushing up his glasses.

"Yes, I'll give her a call." Odile tried not to see Stewart's suggestion as a slight. Maybe he really wanted to see Naomi more than her. After all, Naomi was cuter, more vibrant, and wore shorter skirts. But Stewart was a redhead; why should she care? She placed the call from the red phone box near the

15

pub. Naomi answered and said she'd drive over. Her mother's house was at a distance from the town center.

In the end, the three friends ate an Indian take-away on Parker's Piece, sitting on a blanket from Naomi's car.

"Congratulate me on making that phone call, you two," Odile said.

"Congratulations, but why?"

"It's a long story," Odile said.

"Tell it," Stewart said, taking out his cigarettes and matches. He proffered the pack to Odile and Naomi.

"No, thanks," Odile said.

"No, Stewart. You know you should give those things up. They are so bad for you," Naomi nagged.

"Yes, yes, but I breathe smoke all night in the pub. Quitting wouldn't make any difference." Naomi had no reply to that, so Odile started the story.

"First off, I want to say that everything is different over here. I found out pretty soon that I don't know how anything works: the crosswalks, the trains, the phones. I have been holding my breath since I arrived just waiting for my next disaster."

Naomi laughed her light and bouncy laugh; Stewart heard the pain in what Odile said and looked at her with curiosity and compassion.

"Go on," he said.

"Okay, so I needed a train to Cambridge from London. I go to Liverpool Street station and I buy a ticket to Cambridge. I say 'one way,' and the ticket seller looks at me funny and says 'single to Cambridge' and gives me the ticket. I look at the departure board, see there is a train for Cambridge at platform 4, and I go there. I figure any train from platform 4 will go to Cambridge. When the train gets to Stevenage, a voice comes on the loudspeaker saying, 'All change. This train terminates here. ALL CHANGE.' What does that mean? We don't ride trains in California. I am confused. So I get my bag and step off onto the platform. I go to the departure board, looking for the Cambridge train I am supposed to change to. I can't make any sense of it. A man in a British Rail uniform comes up to me and says, 'So where were you trying to go?' He knows I am lost. 'Cambridge,' I say. 'No more trains to Cambridge today, I'm afraid. Why don't you come into the caff and have a coffee?' I follow him into the station cafe. The radio is playing, 'American Woman,' which I think is ironic. 'Black or white?' he says. 'White,' I say, because I already jumped that hurdle in London." Naomi laughed. "'My name's Reggie,' he says when he brings the coffee. 'I'm Susan,' I say. Sometimes I say Susan because it's just too much trouble to say Odile, spell it, pronounce it, and all that. 'Well Susan,' he says, 'you are only about halfway to Cambridge, but if you wait till five, my friend Len and I can drive you there. I haven't got a car, he does, but he has to get off work at the post office.' Now, I was starting to have visions of being murdered, or worse, by these two, so I said, 'I should probably call ahead to my college and let them know I will be late. They are expecting me'---thinking someone from the college might come to pick me up, or at least Len and Reggie would be deterred from killing me by the fact that someone is waiting for me. So Reggie points me to the pay phone in a booth on the platform and asks me if I have four pence for the call. I say I do and go into the booth. Now, I have never seen a phone like this one. It has a button marked A and a button marked B."

At this point Naomi and Stewart looked knowingly at each other.

"I saw that look. Yes, I put in the coins, dialed the number, the porter's lodge picked up, and I started talking. The porter kept saying 'Hello? Hello? Is any one there?' and hung up. So I tried again. And again."

"You didn't know to push button A to make the coins drop down and complete the other half of the connection."

"Right. What a ridiculous way to make a phone."

"Not really. It comes in handy to save your money if the person who answers is not the one you want to speak to. You just hang up and keep your coins. That's also why some people answer with their phone number. They'll say '6567' instead of 'Hello.' That way you know if you got a wrong number and you can hang up."

"Reggie explained that in the car, but that was after I almost died."

"'Struth! You are one good story-teller, Odile. What do you mean, died?"

"After shouting into the phone my name and my problem, I started to shake and get dizzy. My heart was racing and I couldn't get my breath. I opened the booth to get some air, and collapsed against the door. Reggie came out to help me up. The sound of the blood in my ears was like evil voices shouting, and I had black spots in my vision. He sat me in a chair and told me to put my head between my knees. I was sure I was dying. A lady in the cafe brought smelling salts and put them under my nose. She also put a wet napkin on the back of my neck---I mean a serviette. After a while I calmed down and got some air. Then Len came from work, and the two drove me to Cambridge."

"And they didn't murder you, apparently," Naomi said.

"No, but I thought we would be killed driving at breakneck speed through all those hedgerows in the dark. You English drivers are fearless, driving on the wrong side of the road," Odile smiled.

"You mean the left side of the road," Stewart teased.

"Right. The wrong side."

"Well, ladies, I am off work on Tuesday and Wednesday this week, and I would love to take you both in a punt on the Cam for a tour of the Backs."

"There you go speaking Greek again. What ever does he mean, Naomi?"

"He means he will push a shallow boat with a long pole along the river behind the colleges and narrate what we are seeing."

"I will even bring a bottle, if you like," Stewart sweetened the deal.

Naomi said she had a paper to write and couldn't make it. Odile said yes. She liked Stewart, even if there was no chemistry. He was a nice guy, and maybe she would learn something interesting about the architecture.

3
Fall

"It's supposed to be good luck if you can touch the gargoyle at the center of this next bridge," Stewart said as he gracefully poled the punt along on the river Cam.

Odile was never one to believe in luck, good or bad. She believed you made your own luck by taking charge of your destiny. That go-getter spirit made her want to touch the gargoyle. She would reach out and seize her own good luck. Maybe she wasn't as educated or articulate as all these Cambridge eggheads, but she could do this. She moved to the edge of the wooden seat she was perched on and looked down the river. The gargoyle bridge was still far ahead. She noticed a nun standing in the center of the bridge, with her hand to her mouth, eating something. Just then the breeze caught the nun's white veil and lifted it up around her head like an aura. Odile couldn't help seeing her as an angel.

"Now don't get any absurd ideas, Odile," Stewart said.

And at that moment, Odile looked away from the nun and saw the gargoyle looming. She stood up in the punt, extended her arms, lost her balance, and fell into the cold water.

At first she flailed with her arms, and her head was visible, face turned upward, gasping for air, but then she sank under the surface of the slow-moving stream. The nun, Stewart, and several bystanders erupted into motion, panic, action, and prayer. Stewart stopped the punt as best he could at the spot where she went down, holding the pole on that side, hoping she would grab hold of it, but there was no sign of her.

Under the water, Odile felt tentacles of river weed wrapping around her ankles. She had not been kicking, but when the weeds enfolded her, she gave up even the idea of kicking, since it was impossible. Her mind went black, and she stopped flailing. Silence replaced the echoing of the water in her ears. She felt no cold. She saw only darkness.

Then she heard a voice say, "You are precious to me. Now live." And instantly she felt herself filled with air, like a beach ball, like a balloon, and she bobbed to the surface of the river. Her hand touched the punt pole and clenched around it.

Stewart maneuvered the pole with Odile clinging, to the river bank where several people lifted her from the river. 'Wee-wah wee-wah' the ambulance siren blared, working its way through the narrow and crowded streets of Cambridge to her rescue. Someone had gotten to a phone and dialed 999. By the time the ambulance crew arrived, someone had wrapped her in a blanket, someone had turned her over to let out the water she had taken in, and Odile was bluish-looking but alive.

"How long was she in there?" the ambulance man asked.

"Maybe three minutes," Stewart said.

"She should be dead."

The nun stepped forward. "We can take her to the retreat house. It's just across the road. We will call the doctor to come evaluate her injuries."

"Really, she should go to hospital."

The word 'hospital' woke Odile. She hated hospitals. Once you entered a hospital you surrendered your freedom. She wouldn't go there.

"No, please don't take me to the hospital. I'm okay," Odile managed to say.

"No, young woman, you are not okay, as you put it. But I have a warm bed for you where you can wait for the doctor. I am Sister Lucy. What is your name, my dear?"

"Odile, O-D-I-L-E."

And for the first time, Odile heard Sister Lucy pronounce her name in the French style: O-deel-uh. She felt an immediate warmth for Sister Lucy and willingly let herself be put on a stretcher and carried across the road to the Old Priory Retreat House.

In the Middle Ages, the Old Priory had been a Dominican monastery complete with refectory, prior's lodge, chapel, monks' cells, and a cloister. When Henry VIII dissolved the monasteries, Sir Hugh Bridgefort bought the property and turned it into a residence. Walls were removed to transform cells into spacious bedrooms and sitting rooms for the family. Stones robbed from the cloister built a great hall and a modern 16th century kitchen. Only two sides of the cloister remained, edging the cloister garden, now devoted to vegetables and fruit trees to serve the retreat house guests.

"Here, bring her to my room," Sister Lucy directed, leading them down the corridor. "I have a spare bed she will be perfectly comfortable in, and I can keep a close watch on her recovery." While the ambulance men and Stewart were lifting the bundled Odile onto the narrow bed, Lucy brought a plain flannel night dress out of her dresser. "I will get her out of those wet clothes and put her in this."

"Well, we will leave you to it, then," the lead ambulance man said, and the two of them took the stretcher and headed out the door. Stewart hung back.

"Perhaps you will excuse us while I help Odile change."

"Of course, I will wait in the hall."

"Fine. Would you be good enough to go down to the kitchen and ask Brother Bede to make a cup of hot, sweet tea? We need to warm this girl up!" Lucy smiled at Odile who vaguely smiled back.

When Stewart returned with the tea, Odile was sitting propped up in the bed, her short hair combed across her forehead, primly buttoned up in her warm nightie.

"I feel like it's my fault you fell," Stewart said. "I shouldn't have mentioned the superstition about the gargoyle."

"I think some undergraduates from Magdalene invented that story to trick their rivals from King's," Sister Lucy said. "Everyone who tries gets a soaking. I see you aren't much of a swimmer, Odile."

"No, I never learned. I really hate getting wet."

"Now, who should we contact about you? Stewart, do you know?"

"Odile is a graduate student at Newnham college. She has a friend there, Naomi. And she's American."

"Yes, the accent gave her away. Will you sit here with Odile while I go call the doctor and the college?" and Lucy bustled her rather plump black-clad body out of the room to the one telephone located in the lobby.

"Don't blame yourself, Stewart," Odile said. "I was just showing off, trying to grab some luck for myself. I saw the nun, and it seemed like she was an angel---telling me it was the right thing to do. I'm going to need good luck if I'm going to make a success of myself here at Cambridge, so I thought I would take the chance."

Stewart took her hand and patted it with his large, freckled hand. The romantic date he had planned hadn't worked out. He had invited Odile and Naomi, hoping to

24

impress them both with his encyclopedic knowledge of Cambridge. When Naomi begged off, Stewart rejoiced that he would be alone with Odile. Well, here he was, alone with her, in a monastery, at her bedside, having pulled her out after nearly drowning her in the River Cam. At that moment, Sister Lucy bustled back in. "The doctor is on the way, as well as your friend Naomi."

"Well, maybe I should go. I have work in a couple hours. I will drop by to check on you tomorrow, all right?"

"Okay," Odile said without much enthusiasm. She was anxious to talk privately with Lucy about her experience in the darkness of the river---especially the voice she heard.

"Right. See you tomorrow, then." And Stewart left the room.

———————————• • ———————————

Instead of heading to work at the Town and Gown, Stewart Fraser sat on a bench overlooking the near-death bridge and tried to stop his heart racing. He had managed to save a girl from drowning. Too bad he couldn't have saved his sister Elsie and his mother and father. The three of them were heading to France for a holiday, and Stewart was scheduled to join them after taking his last A-level exam. He never did. They were all three drowned in a cross-channel ferry accident. Stewart felt guilty about that disaster, too, as if his being on the ferry with them would have made any difference. Shocked and demoralized by the death of his family and all the arrangements and changes that entailed, he never matriculated at Trinity, his chosen college. He wondered what was the point of living, having lost everything and everyone he cared about. He holed up in the semi-detached house he inherited and mourned. After a few years, the savings he inherited ran out, and he went to find a job, ending up as barman at the Town and Gown. He was a good barman, not too talkative and very responsible behind the bar. Though his hair was red, very few customers called him

"Ginger." He wasn't the sort that people kidded. Even those who didn't know his story saw him as sad. He reached a hand under his jumper and took a pack of cigarettes and match box from his shirt pocket. He lit one and took a drag. He checked his watch, deciding to walk over to the Town and Gown early, maybe get some tidying done.

———————●●———————

When Odile's friend Naomi arrived, the drab medieval room of the former monastery lit up with a hot pink mini-dress and slick white go-go boots. Naomi had perched a John Lennon cap on her long, blondish hair and shook Sister Lucy's hand with enthusiasm.

"Oh, you are an angel for saving Odile from death! Odile, what could you mean by falling in the river? Are you mad? See, I should have come along. You need looking after, you do." And she bent over Odile's bed and embraced her friend. Lucy could see that Naomi's fun-loving energy was a good influence on the rather stiff Odile. "I talked to the registrar for you, and she said you can be absent for a week with no penalty. I can get you anything you need from your room if you'll give me your key."

"Yes, thanks, it's there in my purse."

"Naomi, she really needs some clothes. I do have some civilian clothes of mine here, but I am quite a bit stouter than Odile. And she would feel more herself in her own things."

"Do you want any books or papers?"

"I can't think right now of what I need. Just the clothes and some shoes."

"I suppose you want those dowdy twinsets you bought at Marks and Sparks?"

"Yes, please. They are very warm and comforting."

"Warm, maybe, but they make you look thirty-five! I told her, Sister Lucy, that only frumpy middle-aged English women wear twinsets, but she won't listen to me."

Sister Lucy laughed. Naomi left soon, smiling and waving, promising to be back the next day with a wardrobe for Odile.

———————•———

"Thank you so much, doctor. I'll keep an eye on her and let you know if any symptoms appear."

"I will check back next week. Stay warm and rest, young lady. You had a very close call."

"Yes, I will," Odile said.

When the doctor was gone, Odile asked Sister Lucy, "Have you ever heard God's voice?"

Lucy smiled. She knew when she saw Odile fall from the boat that she was meant to rescue her and speak to her about God, or spirit, or love. Odile wasn't wasting any time broaching the subject.

"Do you mean with my ears or with my heart or mind?"

"I don't know what I heard it with, but I heard a voice when I was under water."

"What did it say?"

"It said, 'You are precious to me. Now live.'"

"And then?"

"Then I felt my body filling with air, like I was being pumped up like a balloon, and I floated to the top and was saved. It was not a natural thing. Maybe supernatural. But I don't believe in God, so I am confused."

"You don't have to believe in God for God to believe in you and want you to live. I'll be happy to talk to you about these supernatural things, but we don't have to attack them tonight. Let me show you around the place and get you some supper." Sister Lucy helped Odile up from the bed and took her on a tour of the facilities she might need in the night.

That evening, Odile ate supper from a tray Sister Lucy brought her and retired to bed early. Lucy turned out her light so Odile could sleep. She thanked God for sending her this lost young woman to care for, even though she had plenty to do with her appointment at Jesus College, lecturing on sacred art and architecture. She slid open the drawer of her nightstand and took out a Mars bar, unwrapping it as quietly as she could, and lay down in her narrow bed to enjoy the chocolate under the covers.

Odile woke the next morning to find herself in the room alone. Perhaps Sister Lucy had gone off to give her lecture at Jesus College. She found the clothes she was wearing when she fell into the river, clean and folded over a chair. She put them on and walked in her stocking feet down the corridor, following the sound of sizzling and the smell of bacon that reached her from the kitchen. Stopping at the door to the huge stone kitchen, she tapped on the door jamb. A tall, thin friar with salt-and-pepper hair and a white beard turned around. "You must be the lost American."

"Yes, I'm Odile."

"I am Brother Bede. Say, do you mind buttering that pile of toast over there? I need to keep an eye on the bacon."

Odile went to the long refectory table that stood in the center of the room and began buttering the large, oblong slices of white toast from a slab of real butter on a plate. She felt accepted and needed, being put to work like that by Brother Bede. She was feeling pretty useless just lying in bed in Sister Lucy's room, recuperating, when really she didn't feel sick at all.

"So, if you can't swim, what are you doing out on the river without a life jacket? And who ever heard of a girl from California that can't swim?"

"How do you know I'm from California?"

"Your friend Stewart told me while I was making your tea. He also told me that you were a teetotaler until he gave you some sweet cider to try over at the Town and Gown. That loosened you up a bit."

The warmth and welcome of a few seconds ago dissolved when Odile heard that the men had been talking about her, mocking her for being a non-drinker and for getting tipsy when she had downed three halves of cider. It tasted so good; how would she know the power it wielded?

"You don't have any shoes on. Isn't the flagstone cold on your feet?"

"I don't know where my shoes went."

"I put them over by the boiler to dry, but they are still damp. You could have tried some of Lucy's. Here, do you mind putting these plates on the cart as I fill them? We have a full house of guests, and I need to get these out while the eggs are still hot."

Odile complied, surprised at how soon the warm feeling of usefulness returned after her humiliation. "Don't you have anyone to help you get the breakfast on?"

"No, just me. It's part of my penance for annoying the other friars at our house across the river. They said, 'Bede, you are a pain in the arse. Get out' and sent me here. I'm supposed to learn humility and compassion by cooking for a bunch of rich retreatants searching for meaning in life. So far, no improvement. I'm as cantankerous and prickly as ever."

"You seem okay to me."

"Okay. Okay. You Americans always say okay."

"I guess we do. What do you say?"

"All right, let's go," Bede said, not realizing that he had answered Odile's question, and pushed the cart toward the refectory across the passage. Odile followed, hoping to be useful to Brother Bede.

When she returned to Sister Lucy's room after breakfasting on eggs, bacon, toast and strong English tea in the refectory, Odile found a beautiful journal bound in a blue and olive green paisley print lying on her bed. Lucy said from across the room where she was putting something away in a drawer, "I got you that when I was down at W.H. Smith's this morning. A journal comes in handy when you are hearing from God. It helps to write things down."

"Oh, thank you very much. It's lovely."

"I also got you this," and she handed a mint Aero candy bar to Odile. "Bede seldom gives us a sweet with meals, and I like a little something in the evening. Thought you might, too."

Odile smiled as she took the candy. The thought entered her head that it must have been a candy bar that Lucy was eating on the bridge. "Thank you. This is a brand we don't have at home. I love mint."

"If you want to make a study of the different sweets we have over here, I am your woman!" and Lucy pulled open the drawer of the nightstand to reveal a bumper stash of Aero, Mars, Bounty, Cadbury Fruit and Nut, Maltesers, and several other candies Odile didn't recognize. Lucy laughed at Odile's surprised expression. "Yes, I know, I have a little weakness here. I may be a nun, but that doesn't mean I'm perfect."

"No, and I guess Brother Bede isn't perfect either. He said they threw him out of the friary across the river."

Sister Lucy laughed aloud. "That's what he tells people. Really, he volunteered for the job. He is a little bit disagreeable when he gets overworked, but he is very wise and holy as well. If you were willing, it might do him good to have you to help him in the kitchen. What do you think?"

"You mean for just a few more days? Sure, as long as I have shoes to wear on that freezing floor."

"Naomi is bringing you shoes with your dowdy twinsets this afternoon when her lecture ends," Lucy smiled. "Shall I have a word with Bede on your behalf?"

"Okay. Oh, but don't tell him I said Okay; he hates that American expression." Odile laughed, and Lucy enjoyed the sound of the first laugh Odile had uttered since her arrival.

Naomi had brought the clothes, and Odile sat in the quiet refectory, writing in her journal, wearing a pair of

Levi's jeans and lemon yellow twinset. She liked the color yellow, especially with dark blue denim, and the soft feel of the synthetic knit---wool was too itchy. She liked being in the silence of the retreat house. No radio playing, no TV on, no traffic noise because the stone walls were so thick. She hadn't realized how much noise was in her life until it was gone. Suddenly, she felt like she wanted to stay here forever, in the silence, in the still. In the lobby, the only phone rang with that insistent, loud ringing that English phones make.

"Do you want me to answer that, Brother Bede?"

"No, you may not. I must answer it," he almost shouted, hurrying from the kitchen drying his hands on a towel. She heard him say, "2537, Brother Bede speaking... Yes...Yes, I will tell her." On his way through the refectory heading back to the kitchen, Bede said, "Stewart will not be coming today. Something about workmen at his house."

Odile felt half relieved, half sorry. She wanted the time to write and to read the book Sister Lucy had given her, *The Cloud of Unknowing.* But she liked Stewart, and if she were honest with herself she would say her feeling for him had only grown since she came to the Old Priory. Maybe because he saved her life? Maybe because he made her feel safe, a feeling she seldom had around men. She had no phone number for him. She could call the pub, she supposed. But for now, she returned to her writing.

Dear Journal,

Sister Lucy gave you to me to record the words I hear from God, or whoever that was that spoke to me when I was dead. 'You are precious to me. Now live.' That's what I heard before I inflated. I thought I was living, until that day I sat on the bench after the garden party. Then I thought everything I have been doing is useless and dead. I wonder if that is what the voice means. I don't---

Odile's writing was interrupted by Brother Bede calling from the kitchen.

"Say, you spoiled American, come here and lift a finger to help me."

"Spoiled American? You said Lost American before," she said, closing her book and going to him in the kitchen.

"Yes, but you are not lost any more. You are here. But you are spoiled, like all Americans. I would guess you grew up in a large house on an acre of land with two cars in the garage. You never missed a meal, you had holidays every summer, and went to a posh college where you learned nothing but were given high marks, and now here you are enjoying the beauty of England, doing nothing and being waited on hand and foot. Here, peel these potatoes," he huffed.

"Well, let's see how right you are," she said, taking the knife and struggling to peel the potatoes. "I lived in a three-bedroom house with about ten feet between it and the next house. We did have two cars, but not fancy ones. We took a vacation most summers, driving and camping, visiting relatives. I went to the local state college so I could live at home with my parents. I couldn't face the idea of living with a roommate. They can be annoying and messy. I had three meals a day, cooked by my mother, unless she got TV dinners and we ate in front of the television. I studied modern languages, and I think I learned something because I can speak French, Spanish, Italian, and Russian, pretty fluently. I am in England to get a master's degree in international relations, hoping to work in foreign service or at the UN. If that makes me spoiled, I admit it."

"Hmm. Well evidently no one ever taught you how to peel potatoes."

"At home we have a slotted peeler thing. I know how to use that."

"You mean one of these?" he asked, handing her a potato peeler with a bleached wooden handle.

"Yes. That's it. I will make quick work of these potatoes now." Bede laughed.

"See what I mean? Spoiled."

Odile then experienced the simple joy of working side by side in silence with another person. Bede was mixing bread dough, and she was peeling at the sink. Sounds of spoon against bowl, potato splashing into water, peeler hitting the surface of the potato. No words. Just peace and work. She felt her heart swell, and she glanced at her hands in the cloudy potato water to see them shining with a glow. It didn't come from the ceiling light; the kitchen was rather poorly lit. It didn't come from the window; the day was gray. It shone right on her hands, illuminating them like a spotlight on a stage performer. And behind her left shoulder she heard in her ear a voice say, 'Feed my sheep.' She let out a soft "oh." The glow dissipated.

"I hope you didn't cut yourself," Bede said from across the kitchen.

"No, I'm okay. I am done now, Brother Bede, and feeling a little tired. May I go?"

"Yes, you spoiled American. See you at supper." And Odile took her journal and hurried to the safety of Sister Lucy's room.

4
Voices

That evening in her room, Sister Lucy looked over her packet of plain chocolate digestives and said, "Odile, have you heard any more from God?"

Odile looked surprised. "How did you know?"

"What did he say this time?"

"He said 'Feed my sheep.'"

"Would you like to know why I am a Roman Catholic nun?"

"Yes, I would. I just assumed you were raised Catholic."

"Oh, no. I grew up in a wealthy family in Devon, overlooking the sea in an ancient stone cottage. My mother had inherited money, and my father was a banker. I was raised a Methodist, and my folks had no love for the 'RC church'. Even the Church of England was too popish for them. Well, my degree was in art history, and after leaving university I went on a Grand Tour of Europe to see the art.

It was the happiest month of my life to date. In Italy I had a strong internal sense that I had come home. I felt welcome in all the big churches and little churches. I went to see the religious art, but it was the feeling that kept me. I would sit for an hour in an empty church, glued to the pew, rapt. One day I was sitting like that in the basilica of Santa Maria in Trastevere, and I had a vision of the Virgin Mary. She was standing right before me with her hand beckoning to me."

Odile was surprised that she accepted her friend's account without hesitation. She didn't think Sister Lucy was lying or crazy or exaggerating. "Did she speak to you?"

"Her heart spoke to mine without words. I felt overwhelming love, peace, and welcome. It was an invitation to a new life, a new way of being. I realized that all those silent hours I spent sitting in churches were hours of prayer. My soul was praying for God to claim me, and Mary came to take me to him. At least that's how it seemed to me."

Odile felt a stinging heat in her eyes and realized she was on the verge of tears. "That feeling of love and peace---that's what I felt under water...and today."

"Today? What happened today?" And Odile told her about the spotlight on the potatoes. "Odile, I think it is quite clear that God is after you. Time to think about how you will respond."

"Are you saying I should become a nun?"

Sister Lucy laughed. "No. That was the choice I made---and got disowned by my parents in the bargain. Every calling is unique to the person. 'Feed my sheep' could mean so many things. I doubt you are being called to become a professional chef, though it's possible. When Jesus told Peter to feed his sheep, he was being metaphorical, as I expect he is being with you."

"So how can I know?"

"You can pray. You can listen to your heart's movements and responses. You may not know for sure, but you can rest assured that God is sparking some change in you."

"But, Sister Lucy, I don't know how to pray. I never went to church. I don't know God at all."

"He knows you, though. Do you know the Bible?"

"I had a book of children's Bible stories---Moses, David and Goliath, Noah, Christmas, and Jesus loving the little children. I have never opened a Bible as an adult."

"Let me mark a few key sections for you to read. Each night we can do a little Bible discussion."

"Okay, that sounds good. But what about prayer?"

"We can start that right now. After I realized that sitting in silence is a kind of prayer, I started reading up and asking questions, and I found the Cloud Prayer. It is a good place to begin praying if you want to strengthen your connections to God. Now sit up straight in your chair, uncross your legs and close your eyes. Breathe in a few deep breaths and focus your mind on silence. When ideas or images arise in your mind, just let go of them and call up a word that states your intention or willingness to allow God in. I believe he is already inside us, but we stop him acting by our resistance. We will sit like this for 20 minutes or so. When thoughts come, let go of them."

"That's prayer? I thought you had to say words, asking God for something or thanking him."

"This is a kind of prayer. Saying words out loud or in your heart is another kind. Are you willing to try the Cloud Prayer?"

"Yes, but what will happen?"

"Probably not much. You may see darkness; you may see colors. Just let go of any images and let God have his way. It's a kind of surrender."

"Oh, no. I don't like that idea. I have been holding back from surrender my whole life."

"Most of us have. If anything about the prayer makes you uncomfortable, you can open your eyes and return here. Ready?"

"Okay. I'll try."

"No, don't try. There is nothing you have to achieve or prove. You can't be good at it. Just relax and let it happen, whatever it is."

"Okay," Odile said and sat in silence with eyes closed in the former monastery cell with Sister Lucy. Twenty minutes later, Sister Lucy rang a small bell, and it was over. Nothing happened. There was color, then there was darkness, then there were other colors. She felt nothing but silence and peace, a peace that made her feel stronger and healthier. She couldn't explain it. From then on, Odile and Lucy prayed in silence each night in their room. Odile sometimes prayed alone in the chapel during the day. The more she prayed, the easier it got, and the more peace she felt. No fireworks went off. No clouds parted. But the peace alone was worth the time she spent.

Dear God,

I started off calling you Dear Journal, but I really am doing this writing to get closer to you, God, so I might as well address you directly. After Sister Lucy taught me what she calls the Cloud Prayer, she gave me a small book called The Cloud of Unknowing by an anonymous English monk. She got the name "Cloud Prayer" from this book because the writer says there is always a cloud of unknowing between you and me, and that I should beat or batter on the cloud with my prayers and entreaties and that maybe you will let me get closer, little by little. I need to keep my mind open to you like an open door, but a door with a screen on it to keep the bugs out! The bugs are the thoughts that keep coming into my mind when I am sitting in silent prayer. The book says I will mostly see darkness, and that is true. I feel like you are just on the other side of the darkness---so close but so far away. But I need you, and I want to know you. This stuff is all new and strange to me, but I can feel your love just on the other side of the darkness. Please help me to persevere in my prayer. Amen.

5
Scrub

"Brother Bede, can I help you sweep?" Odile asked, coming into the kitchen the next day.

"Okay!" Bede said with a twinkle in his eye, and handed her the broom. "Do you mind telling me more about your family?"

"There's not much to tell. I probably got my brains from my dad. He could have used his GI Bill to go to college after the war, but he spent it on flying lessons instead. My mom wasn't academic, but she was good at math, so she became a bookkeeper. I was the first in my family to go to college. I am still trying to prove myself. They tested me as a kid and said I had a high IQ, but success hasn't come to me yet. For example, I wanted to attend one of the traditionally male colleges here, but even though they are taking women now, I could only get into Newnham. It's like the doctor who told me I would grow to be six feet tall. I fell six inches short of that promise. I always fall short. I hope that studying abroad will give me the prestige I deserve."

Bede huffed. "What about the town where you grew up?"

"Progress, California. Hot, dry, and smoggy. For a couple months of the year, in winter, the hills turn green with grass, but the rest of the time they are brown. There are tall mountains on one side of the valley, but you can't see them on the smoggiest days. They disappear in the brown haze. Nothing like England with all this green and water."

"Yes, we have water," Bede said while he placed rounds of dough on a baking tray for scones. "What do you want most in life?"

"I want to fulfill my destiny and be acknowledged for my achievements."

"Do you want to be loved?"

"Everyone wants to be loved. But I am focused on my career right now."

"Do your parents love you?"

"Yeah, I suppose. But they don't count."

"What can you possibly mean by that?'

"They have to love their child. It's a given. It doesn't really prove the child is worthy."

"Worthy?" huffed Brother Bede, his face turning dark and his posture becoming upright and formidable. "I think you need some scrub therapy, my spoiled American. Give me that broom and I will get you the bucket," and Bede brought her a bucket of smelly disinfectant water, a rag, and a scrub brush. "Now, get down on the floor and scrub these stones until you rethink what you have said about your parents' love." And he turned on his heel and went out into the garden. Odile faced the bucket, startled by his abrupt anger.

Kneeling on the cold stone floor, she took a brushful of water and began scrubbing, like she had seen Cinderella do in the movie. What could he mean by 'rethink her parents' love'? Dismissing the idea as a quirk of that cranky friar, she just kept swishing, scrubbing, and mopping with the rag, moving over a foot or two as she progressed. The rhythm of the task took over; her mind calmed as her body worked. No thoughts, just swish, scrub, mop. And suddenly she saw her mother kneeling on the floor of their house in Progress, scrubbing the linoleum. She saw her dad coming through the back door after a long day at the aircraft factory, lunch box in hand, haggard and spent. And she was inside the heart of her mother and her father. She felt their love for her. She felt how she had hurt them so many times over the years with her sass and her distance. Unbidden, a sob escaped her throat and tears came into her eyes. She sat back on her heels and saw the legs of her jeans soaked with the dirty water. She cried out loud for the first time in many years for the way she had treated her parents' love. Then she heard a voice over her left shoulder: "Arise, my love, my fair one, and come away." She looked around to see who had walked in on her, and there was no one. Leaving the bucket and rag, she fled to the chapel. She felt in desperate need of prayer.

Brother Bede caught her in the corridor outside the chapel. He had a book in his hand.

"Brother Bede, I am so sorry for what I said. I have rethought my parents and their love."

"Good. Now here is a book for you, *The Practice of the Presence of God*. It's by a friar who worked a lot in the kitchen, Brother Lawrence. I know Sister Lucy is teaching you that 'Cloud Prayer' of hers, but there are other ways to be with God. Read it," and away he strode to the kitchen.

———————— ● ————————

Odile had changed into dry jeans and was reading Brother Lawrence on her bed when Naomi and Stewart came to her door.

"Knock, knock," called Naomi, "can Odile come out and play?"

Odile's heart filled with a warm pleasure at the sound. "Yes, what shall we play?"

"We were thinking maybe a paper of greasy chips and a talk on a bench. Nothing too strenuous for the invalid."

"Okay, sounds good to me," Odile said, jumping up from the bed and leaving the book open-face on the pillow. Stewart trailed behind, feeling superfluous when Naomi was bubbling over.

Paper cones of chips in hand, they sat on a bench opposite King's College Chapel. Naomi and Odile had salt and vinegar on their chips; Stewart liked HP sauce.

Odile shared with her friends the morning's events and surprised herself by not editing out the tears of regret. For some reason she didn't need to hide from these friends the way she had always done before. She could feel herself changing and was unsure how to act.

"Do you two go to church?" Odile asked.

"Of course. Church is lovely," Naomi cooed.

"Not since my family died," Stewart said. And Stewart told them the tale of the accident.

"But, Stewart, don't you think it would help you deal with the pain?" Naomi asked.

"No. Church is dead to me."

Odile was stung by the vehemence of Stewart's reply. "You don't mean that God is dead to you, do you?"

"To me they are the same thing," he said. "Can we change the subject?" And he took out his cigarettes and lit one.

Odile wiped her greasy fingers on a serviette. "Okay, why do you Brits call these chips, and I call them French fries? And what I call chips, you call crisps? And why do you put vinegar on them when I put ketchup? And why do you drink Coke warm?"

Stewart laughed. Odile had lightened the mood with her absurd questions. "Are you up for a walk? We can cut through to the river. I need to be at work in an hour."

"Sure. I am not sick. I just like living at the priory better than at Newnham. I feel more alive there. Let's walk."

———————— • ————————

Brother Bede's 'speciality' (with an extra British syllable) was shepherd's pie, which Odile had never tasted but enjoyed. In the evening, Odile and Sister Lucy prayed silently then broke out the sweets.

"How was your lecture today, Lucy?"

"Very fine. I was talking about the structure of the medieval cathedral and how it tells God's story in its very construction."

"Really? I'd like to hear that lecture myself. Is there a cathedral in Cambridge?"

"No, the nearest is in Ely. It's only a short distance. Maybe Naomi or Stewart could take you to see it."

"Naomi might, but probably not Stewart. He is off the church since his family was killed."

"Oh, dear. Great loss tries one's faith and sometimes kills it. I was secretly hoping you and Stewart would hit it off, but a non-believer matched with a mystic like you is a stretch."

"Mystic? How do you mean?"

"Well, Odile, I see you as a mystic because although you don't attend church, you communicate directly and intimately with God. He speaks to you in words from scripture that you don't even know, and he is calling you strongly to be his."

"So you are sure those voices are God?"

"I can't be sure, no. But in my experience, the aura or feeling sense that is left after hearing God's voice is indicative. If the fruits of the Spirit---peace, joy, patience, goodness--- remain, it is probably God. If fear, confusion, anger, or pain remain, it's probably not."

"What if the voices are saying mean, hurtful things?"

"Have you heard such voices?"

"Yes, all the time, but they are not the same voice I heard under water. They are cruel, always tearing me down."

43

"Can you remember the words?"

"Failure. Never amount to anything. You can't do it. You are weak. You are stupid. You are an impostor. Give it up now before you make a fool of yourself. Who do you think you are? Repeated over and over."

"Oh, yes, I know those fellows. Saint Teresa of Avila called them reptile voices, but I just call them lizards. When you finish *The Cloud*, I will get you her book."

"Are those voices Satan?"

"Maybe. Or your own fragile ego trying to stop you from growing and changing. Have they gotten worse here in England?"

"Yes. I didn't hear them so much at home."

"They are apparently threatened by your venturing across the sea and coming to a city with so many religious roots. Teresa said she was gratified when they attacked because they did so when she got closer to God. She would just invoke the name of Jesus and tell them to begone."

"Should I do that?"

"I think it's advisable."

"Sister, is this a Bible quote: 'Arise, my love, my fair one and come away'?"

"Oh, yes. 'The Song of Solomon'. Did Stewart say that to you?"

"No, I think it was God again, while I was scrubbing the flagstones."

"You must have made Bede mad if he set you to scrubbing."

"He called it 'scrub therapy.'"

"Did it work?"

"Yes! I had a vision of my parents and how much they love me. I cried. I was so sorry for hurting them."

"So who do you think was asking you to arise and come away?"

"God, for sure."

"And what kind of language was he using?"

"Romantic language, like a lover would use to his girl."

"So what does that tell you?"

"That God is my lover? That sounds wrong."

"Well, no matter how it sounds, it is true. I see you are reading Brother Lawrence."

"Brother Bede gave it to me and said, read it."

Lucy laughed. "I would like to challenge you to combine what you read in Brother Lawrence with the idea that God is your lover, and see what ensues."

"Okay....Sister Lucy, I have something else to say. In the few days I have been here, I have lost all interest in finishing my degree. My whole goal was to show off and make a big success, but now that has no appeal for me. I don't want those things. I want to just pray, read, and be with God and people who love God."

"That is quite a manifesto. I think you should pray about it---and this time I mean hold the question in your heart as you sit silently and listen or feel for the answer God sends. Still silent, but hold the image of your question in your imagination and wait."

"And if nothing happens?"

"Wait more. Scrub the floor more. Read more of the Bible. Sit in the chapel in silence. Then go ask Brother Bede. He is a whiz at discernment. It's really uncanny."

Dear God,

Really, God, what is going on with me? I never fell when I was at home, but here I keep falling. I managed to keep myself clean and dry at home, and here I keep getting wet in dirty water. At home, I knew how things worked, and I could control my life pretty well. Here I don't know how to do the simplest things like cross the street. I keep messing up, falling, crying. Please tell me, if you can, what all these things have to do with you and the fact that you are 'after me.' Lucy says to 'pray about it'---whatever that means. Is this a kind of prayer? I am talking to you. But how will I hear your reply? Maybe a few minutes of silence. Back soon.

Okay, God, now that was weird. I heard you say 'spotlight' and when I opened my eyes and looked at the paragraph above, I saw the word 'control' in a spotlight like the one you shined on the potatoes. Are you saying I am a control freak? Let me pursue that idea, with your guidance.

I remember in junior high, I signed up for art class, and the teacher started us off with watercolor paints. I hated them. All I got was big, blurry blobs of color. I insisted on being sent to my counselor to change to homemaking class. I liked sewing better because I could control the sewing machine with my knee against the controller. I couldn't control the watercolors, and I hated it.

About that same time I cut my hair short. I hated how I could never make my hair do anything I wanted it to do. So I cut it very short. I was shooting for a Twiggy look, but ended up with more of a Beatle cut. I liked never having to worry about it, but I see now that being in control is a large part of it.

Having short hair, no make-up, and dowdy clothes gave me control in another area: dating. No one gave me a second thought, so I didn't have to deal with boys and their messy demands. The same thing with drinking when I was in college: I always opened one beer and carried it around all night so people thought I was drinking and left me alone. I never got drunk, never lost control, and never got in any trouble. If I did by some chance get asked on a date, I often told the boy I would meet him at the theater or the dance, and I drove myself in my mom's car so I had control of how soon I left the event and where I went after, which was home.

Even living at home during college gave me control: little changed and I took no risk of having an obnoxious room-mate. And the job I had for two years after college: copy editor at the Progress Bulletin newspaper. I earned enough to go to grad school and spent my days at a desk, controlling other people's writing---putting things right, correcting their errors. God, I see what you are trying to say to me. I love to be in charge, don't like taking risks, and have to control.

But what about that night with Trevor? He took control of me then. Oh, no, I don't want to talk about that. Maybe later.

I do need your help with a big decision, though. Where should I go now? If I drop out of Newnham, I will lose my student visa and have to go home. I don't want to go home. Here is where I met you and where you spoke to me and taught me. I don't feel called to be a nun, though. If you want me to be a nun, send me a message.

You already told me: Now Live. How have I not been living? I have been controlling, not living. You are saying I should give up being in control and let life happen to me---like drinking hard cider and standing up in punts and eating greasy chips in paper. Oh, my dear God, I see what you are up to. You are after me. Pursuing me at every turn. Oh, how fun! Can't wait to see what happens next. Amen.

6

Pomegranate

Gray rain greeted Odile when she looked out the mullioned window of the room she shared with Sister Lucy. More water. She headed to the kitchen in search of tea. Brother Bede wasn't there, so she filled the kettle and plugged it in herself. Maybe he was out in the garden.

"Good morning, Odile," Brother Bede called from the garden door, "I was harvesting the pomegranates. Got a sackful of them."

"What do you do with them? My grandma made jelly."

"I make pomegranate cordial. It is our gift to the bishops. What's left, if any, we enjoy with our guests at Christmas. Would you like to help me?"

"Yes, but would you like to join me for a cup of tea?"

"Of course," the stately friar said. "I could stand to warm up my hands." So Odile and Brother Bede sat across from each other at the long kitchen table, cozily sipping their tea.

"Brother Bede, may I ask you something?"

"Something deep and personal, I hope."

"Well, yes. Sister Lucy says you are a 'whiz at discernment.' What did she mean?" He took a sip and looked at her over his cup.

"On several occasions, I have seen or discerned the best career move or calling for a person I spoke to, sometimes total strangers. I don't talk about it since it seems too much like a parlor trick, and like our Lord, I shy away from working wonders to amaze people."

"Well, could you work a parlor trick for me? I suddenly have no desire to pursue my master's degree, and I am feeling lost and rudderless."

"You are certainly not rudderless. What has God told you so far?"

"Have you been talking to Sister Lucy?" Odile asked, thinking they had been gossiping behind her back.

"No, but you have been doing a lot of silent prayer, and I hope you have been talking to God in a friendly way as Brother Lawrence suggests, and it is a fair assumption that he has talked back."

"He has said, 'You are precious to me. Now live,' 'Arise, my love, my fair one, and come away,' 'feed my sheep,' and 'control.'"

"Control?"

"He shined light on that word, like a pointer, so I would reflect on it."

"Ah, yes. Words and light---two of his specialities. Water's another one."

Odile smiled, "He's been using water, too."

"Indeed. Odile, I suggest you keep praying, writing, reading and working. I have no insight to share right now, but I will also pray, and I will let you know if Our Lord shows me anything. Speaking of water, let's get busy on the pomegranates." Bede dumped the fruits from the sack onto the long table. "I will open them, and you can seed them, under water."

"Under water?" Odile felt a fillip of fear, remembering the last time she was under water.

"Mmm-hmm, don't worry, my little American. A bowl of water, not a riverful." Bede filled a large bowl with water, cut a pomegranate in half, and dropped the halves in the water. "They squirt red juice all over if you try to do it above water, so keep them under while you loosen the seeds with your fingers. Let them fall to the bottom and drop the husks in the bin."

"There are references to pomegranates in 'The Song of Solomon.'"

"Of course. They are fertility symbols and symbols of hospitality in that love poem," Bede said, "Very erotic."

Odile was taken aback. "Okay, let me at 'em!" Odile said and dipped her hands in the bowl. Popping the seeds from the husks was easy, and the feel of the seeds smooth and pleasant. A couple times, she forgot and lifted the pomegranate above the water, anointing herself with red drops on her face and apron. Luckily she was not wearing her lemon yellow twinset. Brother Bede sliced all the fruits open, and the table top was covered. Odile worked until her fingers were wrinkled and her back ached. Finally, they were all seeded. "This ought to make a couple barrels of cordial," she said to Bede, who was busy at the stove.

"From your lips to God's ears. More likely a couple gallons, after we add the sugar and the spirits. Thanks, my dear. You just saved me from a job I dislike. You shall have the first taste of the cordial at Christmas."

"If I am still here."

"No parlor tricks, but I have a strong feeling you will be here."

"I hope so. I love it here, Brother Bede, and I love you and Sister Lucy, and God, and everybody," and the tears started flowing. She was about to flee to her room when the voices started shouting in her mind: 'Impostor. Liar. Failure. Phony. You don't love anybody, and no one loves you.'

"Oh, no," she breathed as her knees started to buckle. "The black spots."

Brother Bede put his strong arm around her and walked her toward the garden door.

"Some fresh air, I think. Count to five as you breathe in, Odile, then count to five as you breathe out. Let's take a walk in the garden."

"It's raining."

"Yes, isn't it wonderful? Feel the drops on your face, your hands. Do you feel it? Yes. Now let's sing. Do you know 'Henry the Eighth'?"

No answer came from Odile who was focusing on the rain drops on her face. She could hear nothing over the roar of hateful voices in her ears. Her knees were firmer, though, and the voices were receding.

"Ready, go!...I'm 'Enery the Eighth, I am...'" sang Bede, "Come on, Odile, you know it."

And Odile started singing the silly Herman's Hermits song as Bede walked her around the garden in the rain. As her singing got stronger, the voices faded and the fit let up. She was belting the lyrics out at the top of her lungs as they rounded the far cloister and approached the kitchen. The two of them laughed at the sight they probably made---a soggy friar and a soggy spoiled American singing about Henry the Eighth in the remains of a monastery that very monarch had destroyed. Ironic. Absurd. Wonderful.

"Off with you to get out of those wet clothes. Supper at six."

"Okay, Brother Bede. Thanks."

"Okay, Odile!" Brother Bede laughed and turned to his cooking. His love and wisdom had cut short Odile's lizard attack.

The rain had washed the sky sunny and blue, and the next day Brother Bede sent Odile out in the garden to pick up fallen fruit from under the apple and walnut trees.

"Fresh air and sunshine are the best medicine," he said.

She kept humming 'Henry the Eighth,' hoping it would keep all hurtful voices at bay. As she carried the burlap sack to hold the fruit she picked up, she rejoiced in her life and the gifts she was receiving. Under one of the currant bushes, all alone, grew a tiny white flower, close to the ground, simple and exquisite. Odile stopped her work and gazed in reverent awe at the flower. She wondered at the amount of beauty God had spent on such a small creation, and she hesitated to compare herself to the flower in God's heart. At that moment, the flower spoke to Odile's interior ear. It said, 'I am a powerless flower. I have no control. I am happy.' Stunned, Odile silently thanked God for another communication. He was indeed 'after her' and persistent, too.

"Odile," said Brother Bede as he approached rather solemnly from the kitchen side of the garden, "Come sit with me on the garden seat. I have news."

Her heart sped up in anticipation of what Bede would say. "I have been praying and listening since yesterday, and I have something to share with you."

"I am ready to hear it, after what the flower said." Bede looked puzzled. "I have just been communing with a tiny flower over there, and she gives good counsel."

"Indeed. Well, here is what I saw of Odile Travers: a young mother standing at a bus stop, umbrella stroller over one arm and an infant on the other. Smiling a bittersweet smile." Bede looked at Odile's face and found it inscrutable. It was blank, then turned red, then crumpled into tears.

"I can't, Brother Bede, I can't," she cried, and hurried from the garden.

7
Confession

Sister Lucy had returned earlier than usual and was reading with a handful of Maltesers at her desk. Odile didn't try to hide her state from Lucy and threw herself on her own bed, distraught.

"Tell me," Lucy said.

"I took your advice and asked Brother Bede to discern something for me. He sees me as a mother!" More tears. "And it's impossible. How could he see that? It's impossible."

"Explain," Lucy said.

Odile hung her head and mumbled, "I don't have periods. I haven't had one since I was raped." She barely registered that this was the first time she had used that word to describe her experience. She had never let the word 'rape' form in her mind. Now she did. She cried more, almost from relief.

Lucy took Odile in her arms and let her cry. She murmured, "It's all right. All will be well. God has you. Have you written about this in your journal?"

"No. I started to, but then I quit."

"Do you want to tell me?"

"Yes, I do." And after wiping her nose and composing herself, she took a deep breath and revealed the secret she had kept for five years. "The week before my high school graduation, I accepted a date from Trevor Alcorn. It wasn't my first date. I had gone to a school dance with one boy and dinner with another, but there was no chemistry. After that, I turned down all invitations from plain-looking boys. They just had no chemistry. I was pretty sure a more attractive boy would be better, so when Trevor called, I accepted. He was tall, dark, and drove a shiny new Pontiac GTO his dad had given him for his 18ᵗʰ birthday.

"I put on a sundress and sandals, did my full make-up routine of eye shadow, mascara, and pale lipstick, and tapped my short hair with a brush. Really no need to style it. A thorough spray with Avon cologne, and I was ready.

"Trevor arrived a little late and answered a little brusquely when my dad asked him some questions about his post-graduation plans, but I ignored it. I didn't want to prolong the chat-with-parents either. We got in the GTO and drove away.

"He told me that he was surprised that I accepted because I was known to all the boys as 'No- Deal Odile.'" She looked up to see if Lucy reacted to that remark, but the nun kept her face neutral and open.

"Then he said that he needed to stop by his dad's office for something before we headed to the movies. Mr. Alcorn's insurance office was in a row of stucco offices on a side street downtown. I said I would wait in the car. He said I should come in because he wanted to show me something. I followed him, trying to look cool. He told me to sit on the Naugahyde and chrome sofa while he went to get something. When he returned he had two paper cups with orange juice in them. When I took a drink, I realized there was some kind of alcohol in there, too. I thought, drink it; you need to look experienced.

"When Trevor sat down and started kissing my neck, I felt the chemistry. But it was not the way I had imagined it. I wanted to stop him, and I wanted to look cool. When my head bumped against the metal arm of the sofa, it hurt but I didn't cry out. When his thrusts into me cut and burned with the worst pain I had ever felt, I didn't cry out. I held back my screams. I held back my tears. When he was finished, he tossed my panties to me and said, 'Now to the movie!' I said nothing. I consented to him again, silently.

"We saw a comedy I can't recall the name of. He laughed at the jokes and seemed to enjoy himself. I focused on the burning pain that still throbbed down there. The wetness of my panties made me feel filthy and cheap. Was that all there was to it? Pain, humiliation, and mess? And then a wave of new panic swept over me: what if I got pregnant?

"He left me on my front porch and said, 'Thanks, Odile---and happy graduation!' before trotting back to his shiny new car. For the next three days, I prayed to the God I didn't believe in that my period would start. It never did. That was over five years ago."

Odile looked up at Lucy who took her hand and patted it. Telling someone the story had sapped its power. She felt a weight, a tightness, lifted from her. The two women talked and prayed until late in the evening. At last, Odile got into her bed and asked God to send her a sign of confirmation or negation of Bede's vision. Then she and Lucy slept.

About two in the morning, Odile awoke to a warm gushing feeling between her legs. Oh, no, she thought, I've wet the bed. I shouldn't have had that last cup of tea. Another gush came. She turned on the bedside lamp, and the movement brought another gush. Throwing back the blanket and coverlet, she saw that her night dress and sheets were bathed in dark crimson blood. She drew a breath in shock, and let it out in a shy laugh. God had sent her the sign.

"Sister Lucy," she called softly across the room, "I need you."

Lucy woke immediately, like a mother who hears her child call from a distant room. She came quickly to Odile's side, and her mouth dropped open at the sight.

"Oh, dear. Are you all right?"

"Yes, I feel fine. God sent me a sign."

"That's an awful lot of blood. Do you feel faint?"

"No. For once, I feel far from fainting. I want to jump up and down."

"I don't think that's advisable. We need to clean you up. Do you have another nightie?"

"Yes, I will get it. Do you have some sanitary napkins---I mean towels?"

"Yes, I will get them. You pull off those sheets. Did it soak through to the mattress?"

"It did. I'm sorry."

"Well, beggars for a sign from God can't be choosers of the way he sends it." Lucy chuckled at her own joke, and Odile laughed out loud.

"Thanks, God!" Odile almost shouted. "Let's go tell Brother Bede!"

"Again, not advisable. I have found men to be squeamish about female matters, friars and priests even more so. Let's save it for daylight, and we can phrase it diplomatically."

"I feel bad about the sheets. Let's go to British Home Stores tomorrow and buy some new ones to replace them. I'll carry them out to the dustbin."

"Dustbin? You are becoming so Anglicized!"

"Ha, ha! I know. Or maybe I should keep the sheets as a souvenir, sort of like the Shroud of Turin. You don't just throw away a communication from the Almighty!"

"Now you are getting silly---and heretical."

"I am just so happy, Lucy. I thought I was broken. I thought I was hopeless and I could never have a family. I have always wanted that, and now it seems God wants it too."

"Yes, it does. I've put the sheets in the pillowcase, and we can slip them out tomorrow to the bin. When I am at Jesus College, you can shop for sheets and towels."

"And I will inquire about a new mattress," Odile said.

"After that, you will need to start preparing for your new calling of motherhood. Maybe get closer to Stewart?"

"Maybe," Odile said, and curled up in the big chintz chair under her blankets, cradling her belly like there was already a baby in it. Surprisingly, she slept well till the sun came through the mullions.

Dear God,

I want to thank you for the signs you sent me. The water and the blood. You sent me two baptisms---water in the river and blood in my bed. What does it mean? Baptism is about death of the old life and the beginning of a new life, right? You sure seem to be working on me since I came to England. Why? Why here? Why did you not come after me at home? Was it because I was too sure of myself? Here I am always off-balance. Here I am likely to slip and fall---into a street, into a river. Everything here is different, and I am different. Here I am, beating on the cloud between us, Lord, asking please tell me why. Tell me more. Tell me something. Anything. Amen.

8

Cathedral

"Sister Lucy, may I borrow your lecture notes to take to Ely with me today? Naomi is showing me the cathedral."

"That is wonderful, but you should not take my notes. Let the cathedral speak to your heart today. Let's not get that overachieving intellect of yours in on the act. Keep facts out of it, and let it be a love assignation with your pursuer---God."

"Sometimes you say the weirdest things."

"Don't you remember his seductive word whispered in your ear: 'Arise my love, my fair one, and come away'?"

"Yes, I do. Okay, I will keep an open heart."

"That's all I'm asking."

"We're going over to talk to the registrar at Newnham first. I have to make a decision about continuing my studies. If I drop out, I will lose my student visa, and I don't want to go home yet. I feel that God is not done giving me the English transformation he started."

"If there is any issue with lodging, you are perfectly welcome to stay with me. I like having an American roommate."

"Knock, knock!" Naomi tapped at the open door. She was wearing her black and white vinyl rain coat and black boots. The sky was changeable today, and you never knew what weather might emerge. Brother Bede called it 'samples of weather'---some sun, some rain, some gray. "Morning, Sister Lucy. I am taking your charge on a field trip to Ely today. Tour the cathedral, have tea, and stay for Evensong."

"Oh, there is nothing more beautiful than Evensong in the cathedral. I wish I could come along, but duty calls."

"Right then. We'll be off," Naomi waved, and Odile followed, tucking a folding umbrella in her bag, just in case.

The registrar dampened Odile's spirits. Her three-week medical leave could not be extended, since apparently Odile was no longer ill. She would need to attend and take exams in at least two of her courses to keep her visa. If she chose, she could try to get a work visa from the Home Office, which enabled her to find a job and stay longer, dropping out of her classes.

"Don't let it get to you, Odile. Here, I will cheer you up. We will stop into the play group as we head over to the station."

"Play group?"

"Yes, the redundant church of St. Swithin's on Station Road had been turned into a coffee house and a children's center. They do day care and a mummy-and-me playgroup. I volunteer there one day a week. It takes my mind off my worries, the children are so lovely. Especially Alexander."

"What is a redundant church?"

"Well, church attendance is at a low---actually has been dropping since the end of World War II, and the Church of England has consolidated parishes all over the country and sold off the unneeded (redundant) buildings. They have been deconsecrated, but they can't be demolished because some of them are listed as historical. So, St. Swithin's is now called St. Swithin's Creche Cafe."

"What's a creche?"

"A place for babies---a nursery, a preschool."

"And Alexander?"

"Oh, yes, Alexander. You've got to meet him." Up the steep steps of St. Swithin's redundant church the two friends went and were greeted by joyful voices of shouting children aged three to five. It was play group time, and the chairs around the sides of the space held a rainbow of mothers, young and not-so-young: Caucasian women, Pakistani women, black Caribbean women, and Asian women. Odile was surprised to hear them all talk with English accents. It felt like a true melting pot to her. All of a sudden, Naomi was exclaiming in a shrill voice, "Alexander!" and Odile turned to see a small boy in short pants and suspenders jumping up and down in front of Naomi.

"Miss Nomi! Come and see what I made!" It wasn't Naomi's shift; she worked on Thursday morning, but she followed Alexander to the play table and saw that he had made a tall something out of Tinker Toys.

"Well, isn't that just super! Well done, Alexander. This is my friend, Miss Odile." Alexander extended his small hand and shook Odile's like a gentleman.

"How do you do?" Alexander said, in a serious tone.

"Very well, thank you. I am happy to meet you," Odile said, her heart melting inside her. She had to volunteer to work here. She could feel the love about to burst out of her chest for these tiny and amazing humans.

"Well, we must be off. We are going to ride the train to Ely."

"Take me! Take me!" Alexander jumped up, waving his arm over his head.

"Maybe another time. I will see you on Thursday. Bye." And the young women set off on their adventure.

Tickets bought, they found seats inside a compartment with a sliding glass door. The upholstery looked like it had been installed in the 40's, but it was comfortable and private. Odile told Naomi a short version of her baptism with blood and why she was so elated by it.

"Wow. Well, I guess you better start hunting a husband. How about Stewart? He's crazy about you."

"He is?"

"Yes, you silly."

"I don't know. He doesn't fit the image I always hoped for in a man---tall, dark, handsome, athletic, smart. He's only a little taller than me, with red hair, glasses, and I don't know about athletic---though he was skilled at handling that deadly punt."

"Can you hear how shallow you sound? Those are all physical things. What do you want in his soul and personality?"

"Somebody who respects me, who loves being with me, who wants a family, and is responsible enough to raise children."

"And if a man had all that and red hair, would he be in the running?"

Odile felt the sting of the question and looked down.

"Yes, I guess---but there's got to be some chemistry, Naomi, and I don't feel that with Stewart."

"How would you know? Has he touched you? Have you kissed him? You can't judge chemistry from a distance. You have to connect. When we get back to Cambridge after Evensong, it will be a perfect hour to drop in at the Town and Gown for a nightcap. Stewart will be thrilled to see us, especially you."

"I don't know."

"Don't fuss. It's settled. We're going."

"Yes, Naomi." Odile smiled and surrendered to her friend.

The cathedral at Ely sits on a hill, commanding the land all around, and the train station is down in the valley with the rest of the town. Naomi said they should walk the mile or so to the cathedral because of the beauty, and the rain was only light and intermittent. By the time they reached the cathedral, the sample of rain had given place to a sample of bright sunshine, making the stained glass windows glow. Odile had never seen such a building, and though she took the proffered guide-brochure from Naomi, she mostly just stared in awed silence. No wonder Lucy had not wanted to send her lecture notes.

She went into one of the side chapels and sat in front of some candles others had lit. As she stared at the candle flame, her eyes went to the shadow of the flame on the wall, and she saw the wavering heat trails coming up from the flame. They were transparent, invisible, except for the movement. God is like that, she thought. You can't see him, you can't pin him down, but he is definitely there. You know it from the results: warmth, light, movement, change. Thank you, God, for being invisible but always present. Tears were flowing silently down her face, but she smiled at the joy of it. God had said, "Now live," and she felt for the first time that she was living, not waiting to live, not holding her breath. She dried her tears and rose up to explore more of the cathedral.

As she rounded the east end, near St. Etheldreda's tomb, a voice came over the loudspeaker. "Welcome to Ely Cathedral. Please find a spot to sit or stand in silence. At this time of day, we take a moment to pray for God's world with all its suffering and all its joy." And a beautiful prayer in the high Anglican tradition of the Book of Common Prayer, the King James Bible, and the meditations of Cranmer flowed through the cavernous spaces of the cathedral. She felt part of something huge, something important, something real. It was not just her and God, chatting like chums over the kitchen sink. It was her and God and a whole flood of believers, all over the globe. A new light came on in her heart and mind. She was not alone. She belonged. She was loved by people all over the world she didn't even know. They were praying for her. She was praying for them. She had to find Naomi.

Naomi was walking slowly around in circles on a roundish pattern in the floor near the west door. Odile watched for a moment and discerned that her friend was walking on the path of the design, slowly, following its curves as it turned in toward the center. Odile entered the design at its only opening. She walked slowly as she saw Naomi doing, and her steps became automatic and her mind calmed, like it did in the Cloud Prayer. The path seemed to approach the center, then veered away to the other half of the circle. Naomi reached the center and began the return journey. She and Odile passed near each other and smiled. This was the journey---there was one way in and one way out. You couldn't get lost.   Odile felt another new understanding of her destiny. You lived on a path toward God, the magnet in the center, pulling you. You would have to purposely resist the pull to fail in the journey. How comforting. She would succeed at something. She just had to surrender to the pull. Surrender, there it was again. That word.

Naomi waited patiently for Odile to complete her journey. When she emerged, she went straight into Naomi's arms, and they embraced.

"Naomi, I have learned so much today, and none of it was about architecture. Lucy was right---let the cathedral speak."

"You can tell her you walked a labyrinth, too. I bet she has a lecture on labyrinths."

"Walking it, I felt peace like when I do silent prayer. It's magic."

"Nope, it's God, doing his thing. He has so many ways to get to us."

"Sister Lucy says he is 'after me.'"

"He is after all of us, but he wants us to come to him. That happens on the labyrinth. We come to him, willingly."

"I wish Stewart could know that he belongs and is loved."

"You could light a candle and pray that prayer for him right here. See that big tray of prayer candles?" and Naomi pointed to a glowing corner of the transept. Odile went over, took a long match, and lit a candle for Stewart. She also lit one for each of her parents. And one for Lucy. One for Bede. One for Naomi. One for herself, in thanksgiving for all the new blessings that were coming to her. She put a pound note in the donation box.

"I don't know about you, but all this spiritual work is making me hungry," Naomi said. "Let's go to the tea room. What do you say?"

"I say yes. Yes. I say yes to everything from now on!" Odile exclaimed.

"Well, let's not overdo it, but scones and cream---we can definitely say yes to that!"

Tea in the Almonry tea rooms at the cathedral was delicious and elegant, with a view over the cathedral close. Odile was becoming addicted to strong English tea with milk and sugar. They ordered a plate of tea sandwiches: cucumber, egg, and curried chicken, followed by scones with clotted cream and strawberry jam. They ate it all, and asked for a second pot of tea. With time to kill before Evensong at 5:30, they relaxed and savored their good fortune and friendship.

"Naomi, one time you said that you like church because it's 'lovely.' What did you mean?"

"I have been going to church since I was a girl, with my family. We lived in a row of old houses on a poor street in Croydon. We didn't have much. My dad is an accountant, and my mum didn't work when we were young. She does now, at Tesco. But going to the church on Sunday was the highlight of my week, with all the flowers and music and vestments and candles. I had the foundation as a child, but God started meaning more to me as I grew. I don't do all that mystical stuff you do. I pray out loud. I go to church. I sing the hymns. I take the bread and wine. And I know God loves me, so I try to love others. All the ideas of universal love and forgiveness are lovely. No matter how awful and grubby your week has been, Sunday can be clean and holy. That's my view. Now, the Evensong will also answer what I mean by 'lovely.' Let's head over to the choir."

Odile knew from the brochure that 'choir' in a cathedral is a place as well as a group of singers. She and Naomi took their seats in folding chairs placed near the choir for the Evensong service.

"Do you want to tell me anything about the service before it starts?" Odile asked.

"It's basically evening prayer---some readings and some prayers. But Evensong is choral. There are still readings from scripture, but the prayers are all sung by the choir. It's an invention of the Church of England, but it is so wonderful that Christians of all stripes enjoy listening. Like Lucy, I would say shut down your brain and use your heart's ear to experience it. We can come another time if you want to follow along with your intellect. Or we can hear Evensong right in Cambridge at King's Chapel."

"Just keep an open heart," Odile said.

"Right-o," Naomi smiled.

So Odile closed her eyes and took some deep centering breaths, putting herself in a receptive state. When the organ started and the angelic voices soared up into the roof of the choir, she soared up with them. In her heart's eye she saw God as a swirling, dynamic dance of the Father, Jesus, and the Holy Spirit which seemed to her a female spirit, graceful and warm. Transported to a realm of pure love and light, she lost track of time and space. She jumped when Naomi put a hand gently on her knee.

"Odile, we can go now."

"Oh...I was far away."

Naomi smiled and laughed softly, "I see that. Now you know what lovely is." So the young women floated down the hill to catch the 7:00 train back to Cambridge. They didn't talk much, preferring to let the mood linger as long as possible.

"Naomi, where do you go to church? Can I go with you sometime?"

"Of course, Sunday at 10:00. Saint Clement's in the High Street. I will come pick you up at nine. It's a bit of a walk. But now we have to get over to the Town and Gown."

Odile no longer hesitated to surprise Stewart. She had prayed for him in the cathedral; they were forever linked.

9
American Woman

As they entered the pub, Odile heard the jukebox playing 'American Woman.'

"Not that song again!" she exclaimed, and Stewart immediately turned from the bar he was mopping and looked at her, beaming.

"I think I hear an American woman somewhere in the room," he called, and several customers turned to look at her. Embarrassed but pleased with the greeting, she went up to the bar with Naomi. "What will you have, ladies?"

"Two halves of Strongbow," Odile said with confidence. Stewart smiled and went to get the half-pint glasses he used for cider.

"Taking a break in about ten minutes. I'll join you."

"Okay. We will be on the patio for the fresh air."

"Isn't it still raining?" Stewart asked. From the bar he had no view of the pub's river-facing window, only the smoky, dark interior.

"Oh, no. It's clear and beautiful." And the girls waved joyfully as they stepped out on the patio.

When Stewart joined them, he got an earful from Odile about how wonderful the day had been: Alexander at the play group, the beauty of the cathedral, the deliciousness of the tea, and the definition of pure loveliness---Evensong. He had never seen Odile so animated and joyful. She was ravishing to him. He basked in her glow.

"The bad news is that I have to take at least two courses to keep my visa. So, I think I'll keep the Religious Climate course and Comparative Trade Laws. I have a lot of catching up to do, but Naomi has the notes. I surrendered my room to another student who has been sharing with two others. She is thrilled to have it, and she will complete my lodging contract. I'll stay at the Old Priory with Lucy till the Michaelmas term ends; then I'll have to make a decision. But I refuse to worry about it. God will work it all out. And I want to volunteer at St. Swithin's with Naomi. I love those little ones."

"You are so full of life tonight," Stewart said.

And Odile let herself go, not holding her breath, and hooked her hand around Stewart's neck and drew him to her, kissing him on the lips. More than a peck, it communicated more than friendship. The gesture was not lost on Stewart. She already had his heart, and now she had given him hope.

Dear God,

Bang! Bang! It's me, Odile, pounding on the cloud between us. Please open the cloud, Lord, so I can thank you for this amazing day. Lucy said, 'let the cathedral speak,' and it really did. You are real, though invisible, like the candle's heat. You are color and light, like the stained glass. You are music and voices lifted to the skies. You are silence and peace, like the little chapel. You are love and fellowship, like the congregation. And you make me brave. I kissed Stewart. You sent him to me, like you sent Lucy and the others. You are after me, and I am after you, too, God. That is why I keep banging on this cloud. I

know you hear me, though your voice is still. I will keep bang-
ing, Lord. I promise. Amen.

———————— • ————————

When Odile emerged from the lecture on religious
climate at Trinity Hall, Stewart was waiting on the terrace
where students were taking a tea break. Odile felt a thrill
when she saw him.

"What a nice surprise!"

"I thought maybe we could have lunch and I could
walk you back to the priory---carry your books?"

She laughed and took his arm, which he bent
automatically to accommodate hers.

"That would be lovely. Stewart, I have a question for
you. What do you most desire in life?"

"That's pretty heavy," he said as they crossed the road
arm in arm at the green man signal.

"Well, do you want money? Fame? Travel? Children?
I used to think I wanted recognition and power, but now I
don't." Odile felt brave again today, and she didn't want to
act coy with Stewart, the man God had sent her. Stewart
responded with his own candor.

"Odile, I am alone. I have a house, a job, and myself.
I lost my whole family at once. I want to belong to a family
again. I want to live for someone other than myself. That's
what I want. How about you?"

"I don't feel alone any more. I know I belong to
something big and real. But I want to live for others, too, and
I would love that to include children. Something visceral
happened in me when I shook little Alexander's hand, and
I knew I must have children. It was weird but wonderful."
Stewart said nothing. "Forgive me for being so forward,
Stewart. It's not that I am a pushy American; I just feel that I
need to make some steps in the direction of my new calling---
like I don't have all that much time."

"You're still a young woman. You have lots of time."

"I hope so. Where are you taking me for lunch?"

Stewart bought her a hamburger with egg on it and a chocolate milk shake at Wimpy's. The food was totally different from what she would have been served in America, say at McDonald's. She managed to stop herself from using the expression 'back home,' and thanked him graciously. When they reached the Old Priory, Stewart kissed her and went across the bridge to work. Odile went to her room, confessing to herself that Naomi was right. You can't judge chemistry from a distance. But you can judge it from a kiss.

Dear God,

Here's a quote from 'Song of Solomon': 'do not stir up or awaken love until it is ready.' You are stirring it up now. Funny how kissing Stewart has changed the alignment of the planets. You're not just after me, you're after Stewart, too. I feel your pleasure when I touch Stewart. Is that weird? You are my true lover, but Stewart is your stand-in. You have no lips to kiss me or arms to hold me, so you kiss me through Stewart. Is that right? And if you are loving me through Stewart, then you are loving Stewart through me. So there's no reason to hold back. Our love is an extension of your love, and therefore it's holy. Stewart says you are dead to him, but that's not true, is it? You are going to turn him around by loving him through me, just like you turned me around by loving me through Lucy and Naomi and Bede. Am I right? Is this a ray of light you are letting through the cloud that I keep pounding on? Please let it be. Amen.

The next day, Odile found her way to St. Swithin's Creche Cafe and met Naomi on the steps. The children in the play group were having a 'Clay Day'---making things from clay. A grant from the Arts Institute paid for their creations to be fired in a kiln at a local studio, so they needed encouragement to mold sturdy pieces that wouldn't crack in the firing. Alexander was absent today, so Odile sat on one

74

of the tiny wood chairs between two sisters, Maureen and Eileen. The method they were learning was to make a long worm of clay by rolling it between their hands or on the table top, then coiling it up into a dish or ashtray.

"Our father doesn't smoke," Maureen said.

"Well, that is good. You can make a little saucer for him to drop his keys or coins into."

"Our mum keeps her keys and coins in her purse. What can we make for her?"

"How about a dish for her earrings or hair pins?"

Maureen frowned. She decided to make her mum a snail, since coiling up the worms made a rudimentary snail.

While she helped and encouraged the girls with their projects, Odile got the urge to make something as well. She rolled a worm and splayed out the bottom to give it a firm base. Then she rolled a smaller worm to go across it, but the arms drooped. She removed it and made a short, plump cross piece that didn't droop. It looked more like a market cross than the cross of Christ, but it stood on its own. Then she wanted to make a woman, kneeling at the cross. She rolled worms and crossed them to make legs and arms. It was a mess. She thought of her childhood frustration with water colors, but she refused to give up. She tried again. This time the woman looked like a sack of potatoes. The next attempt looked like Medusa. She took a deep breath and prayed in her heart---Okay, God, I am struggling. Please help. Then she rolled out some sturdy worms and made a flat woman with arms out and legs straight. She added an A-line skirt and long hair to make it clearly a woman, though she had short hair herself. Then she saw it. The woman wasn't kneeling. She was prostrate in front of the cross in a posture of humility and surrender. Odile breathed 'Amen' softly and called her work done. The next week when the pottery came from the kiln, the woman had shattered, but the stubby cross was intact. She carried it home to the priory and put it on her nightstand. She would keep it forever.

On Saturday night, Odile and Naomi had a girls' night at the Town and Gown: pub food for dinner and a few halves to wash it down. Naomi chose steak and kidney pie, and Odile ordered fish and chips. The smoky pub was warm and convivial with the conversations of friends and lovers. Naomi went to the jukebox and put in several coins, ordering up the next five songs. As each one came on, she sang along. She knew all the words and tunes, being a dauntless fan of Top of the Pops. Odile, denizen of the silent priory, was falling behind in her pop music awareness.

"Oh, I love this song!" Naomi said, and started singing, "L-O-L-A, Lola." A man came to the table taking Naomi's hand, and she arose gracefully and started dancing with him as if they were Astaire and Rogers, well-rehearsed. Naomi had a shapely body and long, straight hair which she kept immaculately clean and brushed. Her blue eyes had surface lights and smoky depths. Her only visible flaw was her gappy front teeth, but she had learned to smile in a fetching way that covered them. When she smiled, she looked like she was keeping a secret. It drove men crazy. Once she started dancing, she had no lack of partners all evening.

Stewart was hectically busy at the bar, The Town and Gown being one of the last remaining free houses in Cambridge. Stewart had explained that a free house could serve beer from any brewery; therefore, the Town and Gown drew a wide clientele, since they offered Bass, Marston's, Newcastle, and Courage. A 'tied house,' owned by a particular brewery, could serve only the products of that brewery.

Odile saw Stewart cross to the jukebox, put in a coin, push some buttons and hurry back to the bar. After a few more songs played, a slow dance came on, and Stewart emerged from the chaos of the bar, took Odile's hand, and drew her into his arms. Neither one of them knew any dance steps, but they knew enough to hold each other close and sway to the pulse of the music. Odile felt the strength and warmth of Stewart's body. She was safe, and she belonged. She wanted Stewart to feel the same. She looked into his eyes and smiled, and her heart rose up into that smile, communicating the message a woman knows how to convey: I am willing. Stewart's smile held some surprise and much joy. He pulled her closer and kissed the top of her head, smelling her herbal shampoo under the smoke of the pub. When the song ended, he kissed her hand and rushed back to work. His fellow barman looked relieved when Stewart returned, and Odile hovered on cloud nine.

"Maybe we should think about going; we've got church tomorrow," Naomi said as she dropped into her chair, exhausted but exhilarated.

"Okay. Let me just tell Stewart goodbye," and Odile walked boldly up to the bar, worked her way through the crush, and said "Bye, Stewart."

"Bye, Odile. Can you come for Sunday lunch tomorrow? We do a traditional roast with Yorkshire pudding. My treat."

"Sounds lovely. I'm going to church with Naomi. What time?"

"We serve from 12 to 2."

"Okay, see you then," and she waved to her lover as she went out the door.

Dear God,

Thanks for dancing with me and loving me so much last night. I felt your love electrifying the love between Stewart and me. I feel it being stirred up inside me by your invisible hand. Am I right? I am still banging on the cloud, Lord. Open to me. Amen.

10

Baptism

St. Clement's parish church wasn't as grand as the cathedral, but it had an old Victorian organ and a small choir. Naomi showed Odile how to follow along in the *Book of Common Prayer* and the separate hymnal. Keeping both books in her hands or on her lap challenged Odile because she also had to stand up for prayers and singing. The service was active, more than the Evensong had been. After the readings and the sermon, which Odile enjoyed, the prayers started building up to the Eucharist.

Odile whispered to Naomi, "What do I do when the communion comes?"

"Follow me up for communion."

"But I have never been baptized."

"Oh, I think you were---in the River Cam." Odile frowned. "All right. Follow me up to the rail, and cross your arms across your chest like this," Naomi demonstrated. "The priest will give you a blessing but no bread."

As Odile waited on her knees, arms across her chest, for the priest to come to her, her heart yearned for the body of Christ like a homing device. She was part of the Body of Christ, baptized or not, and she craved the food that feeds the Body.

Then the priest had his hand on her head and was saying, "The Lord make his face to shine upon you," and it was over. Her heart cried out, hungry.

Back in the pew, she said to Naomi, "What do I have to do to be baptized?"

"You just have to ask. We can speak to Vicar Tomlinson during coffee hour."

When asked to baptize Odile, the vicar said, "Follow me to the sacristy. Let me look on the calendar." And Odile felt again that she was welcome, that she belonged. God's agent, Vicar Tomlinson, seemed happy to tie Odile into the fabric of the Body of Christ with another thread---the thread of Holy Communion. He gave her a little booklet on baptism and another on the eucharist. She was to read them both and call him at the church number if she had any questions. Two weeks from today, on All Saints Sunday, she would be baptized. Other adults, children and infants would join her, and Naomi would be her sponsor.

As she was turning to leave, the vicar asked, "Odile, is there any chance you have already been baptized?"

"I don't know. I don't think so. Does it matter?"

"Yes. There's a different ceremony if you are already baptized. Could you ask your parents about it? If not, we will proceed as if you are unbaptized."

Odile didn't want to call home to ask about baptism. She was afraid to admit that she now believed in God, that she had been wrong. What would her mom and dad say?

———————————— ● ————————————

A chalkboard sign stood at the door to the Town and Gown: Sunday Lunch---roast beef, Yorkshire pudding, sprouts, mash, gravy, and choice of sweet. Odile came alone, hesitant to assume that Naomi was included in the invitation. She walked in and looked for Stewart. A young woman in black skirt and white blouse asked, "One for Sunday lunch?"

"I am supposed to be meeting someone, so it is two for lunch," Odile said. Just then Stewart emerged from the kitchen.

"There you are! Jenny, let me introduce my friend Odile." The girls shook hands and smiled. "I am taking my long break now to eat with Odile."

"Right," said Jenny, "and will you be having the Sunday special lunch?"

"Yes, indeed," Stewart said, and pulled out the chair for Odile.

Stewart looked handsomer than usual today. He may have had his hair cut or ironed his shirt. Odile was proud to be seen with him.

"Would you let me buy a bottle of wine to go with the meal?" he asked.

"Yes, that sounds nice. I know little about wine, so I will trust your choice."

"So, how was church?"

"Oh, Stewart, it was so wonderful. Vicar Tomlinson is going to baptize me in two weeks. Will you come? Please?"

Stewart took in his breath, but the look of pure joy and anticipation on Odile's face won him over.

"Yes, of course. I hope my presence doesn't cause the roof to fall in before he gets the sprinkling done."

"Me, too, because I have never wanted anything more than that tiny wafer of bread---once I found out that I couldn't have it. It almost broke my heart. The vicar blessed me, but I felt so excluded, not being able to take the bread and wine. Have you been baptized?"

"Mmm, as an infant. Also confirmed as a teenager. I served as acolyte for years. We were pretty churchy, until the accident. Then I chucked it."

"Can you tell me why?"

"Mostly anger at God. But also, after the funeral and the reception after, I never heard a word from any of those church people, except Mrs. Barley who came by once or twice. I didn't go to church, so they forgot me. Out of sight, out of mind. Hypocrites: always preaching love for the poor and outcast and then casting out anyone who is difficult to deal with. But I shouldn't be saying this when you are so high on the idea of becoming a Christian. Every church is different, and maybe Tomlinson's is one of the good ones."

"He made me feel very welcome, and it's Naomi's church, and she likes it, so..."

At that moment the lunch arrived and the bottle of wine, so they started the meal.

Stewart said, "Oh, do you want to say grace?"

"I am such a new Christian, I don't know what to say."

"I'll do it. Lord, bless this food we are about to eat, and strengthen us in your service. Amen."

"Thank you, Stewart." And Odile felt a rush of love for Stewart who had made this small sacrifice for her sake. God was after him, too. She took her knife in her right and fork in her left, as she had learned here in England, and tasted the Yorkshire pudding in gravy. "Oh, my. That is heavenly."

The whole lunch was heavenly, including the rhubarb crumble with custard she chose for 'sweet.' Stewart had the trifle. They were well fed and mellow from the wine. The October days were getting shorter, and Stewart walked her back across the green to the priory in misty, fading sun. They held hands. Where did they go from here? Odile wondered. She did not want to play hard to get since she would not be hard to get at all, if he wanted her.

Dear God,

I am so yearning to take in your body and blood. When I could not take communion today, I was angry. But I will be baptized in two weeks, and then I will have you. I saw what you did there with the table prayer--- having Stewart say it. Beautiful! On Wednesday, I am going to help Stewart at his house with some redecorating. But before that, I have to call home. I am dreading that. Please give me strength. Amen.

━━━━━●━●━━━━━

Odile stepped into the red phone box and pulled the heavy door shut. Her hand shook as she dug the coins from her purse and laid them on the shelf by the phone. Inserting the amount the operator required into the slot, she prayed for the ability to keep her voice controlled. Her mother answered, sounding sleepy. Maybe Odile had underestimated the time difference.

"Hello?"

"Hi, Mom, it's--"

"Odile! What's wrong?"

"Nothing's wrong. Everything's fine."

"I thought we told you to write, not call, unless it was an emergency."

"It's okay, Mom, I just have a question. Was I baptized?"

"Why are you asking that in the middle of the night?"

"I'm sorry. I thought it was morning over there."

"No, you were never baptized. Baptists don't baptize babies, and by the time you were old enough to choose it, we had stopped going to church."

"Why?"

Silence.

"Mom?"

"It's a long story, Odile. You can't afford the long call for me to tell it."

Silence.

"Mom, do you realize that every time I ask you something about God, you don't answer me?"

"That is not true. I taught you the Lord's Prayer. I read you Bible stories. I took you to church on Easter."

"Mom, that was when I was a child. Now I am an adult, and I want to be baptized, and you won't tell me the truth."

Odile could hear her voice becoming shrill, so she took a deep breath and waited through the next silence.

"Something happened, and we just left. That's all. We never went back."

"And you never thought about trying a different church for my sake? You never think about me."

"And when do you think about us? You've been over there for months, and we got one postcard from London and nothing since. Could you maybe let us know how you are doing?"

"Well, I'm letting you know now. I'm doing fine, I'm going to church, and I'm getting baptized, not that you care."

"Odile, we do care. Please don't think that we don't."

"Well, fine. I guess I'll let you get back to bed."

"Okay, Odile. I will write you a letter with the whole story---"

Just then a loud string of beeps indicated that the time on the telephone's meter had run out, and Odile, having no more coins to deposit, hung up the receiver. Immediately, she felt ashamed of herself. Where had all her new godly patience gone?

11

House

When Odile rang the doorbell at Stewart's house, he came to the door in a paint-spattered sweatshirt. Bits of damp wallpaper stuck in his ginger hair, and he already looked exhausted.

"Did you start without me?" Odile asked.

"I did. I hoped to get it done before you arrived so we could enjoy the day."

"We will enjoy the day. I love peeling wallpaper. I helped my grandma peel three rooms in her upstairs apartment---flat---when I was ten."

"Do you want a cup of tea first?"

"I'd rather get right to it. Do you have two scrapers?"

"Here, take this one. It's the sharpest."

And Odile and Stewart attacked the horrid wallpaper in the downstairs front room of his semi-detached house, built in the 1930's. Odile would have called it the living room, but Stewart called it the lounge. His mother had papered all four walls with a dark brown paper covered in orange poppies. Odile was happy to peel it off because of its ugliness, but she knew Stewart's motive was different. He hadn't used the lounge for years because the room reminded him too much of his mother and the loss of his family. He lived only in the kitchen down the hall and one of the bedrooms upstairs. Why he had chosen to work on it now, she did not know. She hoped to find out.

"So, are you going to choose a new paper?" Odile asked.

"No, I just want to paint the room a plain light color. This room is so dark already, facing northeast as it does."

"Well, we better be careful not to gouge the plaster then."

"It's all right. I worked one summer for a painter-decorator and I got very skilled at texturing walls and painting them. I can make these walls look as good as new." Just then Stewart was taken by a fit of coughing. He struggled to catch his breath.

"Maybe you breathed too much of that vinegar water we are spraying."

"Or maybe I should give up working in a smoky pub."

Odile thought to herself: or give up smoking, but she said nothing. Nevertheless, the topic ended their conversation for a while. They worked silently side by side, the only sound the scraping of metal against plaster. Odile was down on her knees working below the bay window that faced the road. Stewart was up on a ladder, working on a section near the ceiling which, thank God, was not papered, only painted. An ocher patina left by years of cigarette smoke yellowed the paint. Both of Stewart's parents had smoked, so they had little objection when Stewart picked up the habit. Like many men who served in World War II, both Odile's and Stewart's fathers had smoked. Cigarettes were part of a soldier's daily ration, after all.

"Maybe I will take that cup of tea you offered. This is thirsty work."

"Right," Stewart said and led her down the hallway to the sunny kitchen. Through the window flanked by net curtains in need of a good wash, Odile saw a small patch of lawn surrounded by flowering shrubs. The chrome table and chairs had blue seats and a blue-and-white checked Formica top. A radio and a toaster stood on the table. No wonder Stewart chose to live mostly in this bright, happy room. Stewart plugged in the electric kettle and set it on the drainboard.

"I hope you like Typhoo."

"I don't know. I just drink what people serve me. I like it all."

"Well, some ladies find Typhoo too strong and will only drink PG Tips."

"La-di-dah," Odile laughed. "The English can be so persnickety."

Stewart smiled and brought the biscuit tin from a shelf. It said 'McVities' on it with a Christmas design, but it contained digestives and Jaffa cakes. The family biscuit tin, it had served sweet treats to Stewart's family for two generations. Odile took a digestive and slumped back against the chair with at sigh. The digestive tasted of orange from sharing the tin with Jaffa cakes.

"After our snack, will you show me the rest of the house? Are you renovating any other rooms?"

"Sure. I'm just doing the lounge right now."

"How long is it since the accident?"

"Seven years."

"And what made you decide to redecorate the lounge now?"

Stewart looked at Odile over his cup. "You did." Her heart leapt, but she kept her face puzzled.

"What do you mean?"

"Since the day you fell in the river, I have felt a change. I all of a sudden have hope. Energy. A desire to live again, not just hole up in one room. I want to make my house presentable to friends, guests. Presentable to you. Maybe ask you to move in some day."

A woman who hears words like these has several choices. She can pretend she never even thought of such an eventuality and play hard to get, maybe act shocked or insulted. Or she can laugh it off as a joke and defuse the conversation. Or she can meet the man's honesty with openness of her own.

"I would like that," she said.

"Was that an answer to a proposal I haven't made yet?"

"Or to a proposition you have made already. Either way, the answer is 'yes'."

"Oh, my God. That was easy," and Stewart leaned across and kissed Odile. She smiled and kissed him back. They touched their heads together and caught their breath. "What is happening to us?"

"I think we are confessing our love. I love you, Stewart, and I want to be with you."

"Shall we marry?"

"Yes."

"And have children?"

"Definitely."

"When?"

"Well, not until we get the lounge redecorated and I am baptized. I want to be able to take communion at my wedding."

"The lounge. I forgot all about it. We can quit for today. We have to celebrate."

"No, we have to finish. We can celebrate later with our friends. Never leave a project half done; you may never come back to it, and then what?" So they put their cups in the kitchen sink and went back to scraping and peeling the lounge walls. Working side by side made them both willing to talk about serious subjects they needed to air.

"Stewart, have you been in love before?"

"I had a serious girlfriend in school, and I was getting ready to ask her to marry me, but then the accident happened. After that, I was so shattered, she went off and married someone else."

"Just like that?"

"No. It was me. She came over often, tried to take me out to do things, but I refused. I felt so guilty and lost. Eventually she gave up. And I just mourned---felt sorry for myself. That's the first time I have put that in words: 'felt sorry for myself.' I want to stop feeling sorry for myself. I want to start a new life with you, my American woman. I want to take care of you and our children, not be so self-centered."

"I see we are two peas from the same pod. Self-centered is me, although controlling is another one of my flaws. I am a perfectionist, and I want to force others to come up to my standards. The problem is they don't, and I don't. Then I think life is disappointing and frustrating."

"I see. That's why you forced me to finish this room, even though I wanted to go out to celebrate."

Odile was taken aback. "Yes, that is exactly what I do. I say 'no' too much. I want to say 'yes' more and let things flow. I always try to turn the river to go my way."

"Well, the River Cam showed you who's boss."

Odile laughed, "I never thought of it that way. You're right." And directing her words to the yellow-stained ceiling, she said, "Thanks, God."

"I think it's cute how you do that."

"I learned it from Brother Lawrence."

"Another one of the friars at the priory?"

"No, a medieval one in a book. He advises us to practice the presence of God by chatting with him in a casual way all day long, so when I see his hand in my life I just thank him. And his hand has been busy in my life since I crossed the Atlantic. You are the biggest of the many gifts he has given me."

"I wish I could believe like you do."

"Seven years is a good time for a big change. Maybe you can change more than the lounge."

"Maybe. I guess God can do what he wants, if he wants."

"Stewart, I want to tell you something very personal, but I'm afraid. Still, if we're going to marry, you need to know."

Stewart came over to Odile and turned her toward him, away from the wall, because he sensed the onslaught of a momentous communication.

"Please, Stewart, go back to the work. I can tell you easier if I'm not looking at you. I will speak it to the wall, and you just listen in. I know I'm being controlling, but humor me, okay?" And Odile narrated the night in the insurance office, the five-year drought of menses, and the baptism of blood that had given her hope. Stewart started to interrupt a few times, but stopped himself. He wanted to give her plenty of space to confess what she needed to confess, to clear the air between them so that they could start a new life together.

"May I comfort you now?" he asked when she said she was finished.

"Yes, please," she said, moving gratefully into his arms and feeling the strong safety of him. Now that the tale was out, the tears came, quiet tears of relief. Stewart let her cry until she was done. He had cried enough in his own pain to know that the hurting person needs release more than advice. 'Now, now, stop crying,' is the last thing they want to hear.

Odile seemed re-animated by her confession and applied herself to the work again.

"Come on, Stewart, just one more wall to go," she said.

"Bossy boots," Stewart said, and pitched in with gusto to rid the room of old ugliness and old memories. In the course of finishing the last wall, the lovers started talking about their plans. Where could they get married? Stewart was for a simple trip to the Registry Office, but Odile wanted a church wedding at St. Clement's, small, yes, but in the sight of God, her true lover.

"If you are serious about this," Stewart said, "I want to do up all the rooms in the house. Luckily, it's a small house, 'two up, two down' basically. My parents slept in the front bedroom with the bay window, but the back bedroom is slightly bigger and has a view of the countryside. I don't think I can afford to modernize the bath, though it needs it. Or the kitchen."

"I like the kitchen as it is. Cozy and warm. Lots of light. We have our whole lives to fix up all the rooms. Even make a nursery one day." The thought of creating his own family thrilled Stewart; he had been so devastated by the loss of his parents and sister. As the sun was setting, they finished removing the last of the paper, very tired and very happy.

"Come through to the drive, and I'll take you home. We can get a bite at the Chinese take-away."

"Okay, and you can come in and we'll eat it in the refectory. That'll please Brother Bede," Odile laughed. And that is what they did. Bede's sharp nose smelled the foreign spices in the Chinese food, and he entered the refectory, ready to fight. When he saw it was his favorite, Odile, he relented, greeted her and Stewart cordially, and returned to the kitchen. He discerned an aura of sacredness in their posture, side by side, and retired reverently. Seeing that his vision of the young mother was probably right, he smiled to himself.

Dear God,

Thank you, thank you, thank you. I am so tired, I can't write any more. Please guard me in my sleep. Amen.

12

Rite

O dile had hoped to wear white on All Saints Sunday, like the babies and children being baptized, but fall was no time to shop for white, and she couldn't borrow from Naomi who was too petite or Sister Lucy who was too stout. From her limited wardrobe she chose a dark skirt and white blouse and her dressy shoes. Stewart would drive her to church, so she didn't need to worry about walking very far in heels. Since the church wanted to emphasize the communal nature of baptism, the whole congregation would be present to support Odile 'in her new life in Christ.' Odile liked knowing that she was joining herself to a universal communion made up of people all over the planet who loved God. Someday, maybe Stewart would feel he belonged. She wanted to tell him how much his presence at her baptism meant to her, but she didn't want to push. 'Let it be,' she said to herself, and God concurred.

After the opening readings and prayers, those to be baptized and their supporters went to the back of the church where the font stood. The priest gave thanks and blessed the water for the ceremony. He began with the smallest child, holding babies in his arms, and lifting children up to the edge of the font where he poured water on their heads using a scallop shell to scoop up the water. One baby cried, the other was silent, the children stoic, and then came Odile. She stood by the font and leaned over.

"Odile, I baptize you in the name of the Father (one scoop of water) the Son (another) and the Holy Spirit (another). Amen"---and all the congregation also said Amen, in unison. The force of the voices entered her body like a wave of strength. She was not alone.

Vicar Tomlinson gave her a linen cloth to dry her hair and face with, and as she looked over his shoulder, she saw Sister Lucy in her black habit with white veil and Brother Bede in his brown robe and sandals. They were smiling ear-to-ear, the love in their faces palpable.

"Let us welcome the newly baptized," the vicar said, and a roar of applause rose up out of the church. Odile saw Lucy clapping, though Bede was not. Applause was not usual in the priory, and he did not approve.

The service continued with the usual Eucharistic prayer, building up to the sharing of the bread and wine. For the first time in her life, Odile would be able to take in the body and blood of Christ, and she shook in anticipation. She had prayed that Stewart would come up, too. He made no move, but as she rose to go forward, she sensed his presence behind her. It would be his first communion in seven years. She rejoiced as he knelt beside her at the rail. She smiled. He smiled. The priest came to them down the row of communicants, feeding them with God.

During coffee hour in the hall, Sister Lucy gave Odile a small gift to commemorate the day. "Now that you are part of the communion of saints, I thought you should have a book of saints. When you get time, be sure to look up your namesake, Saint Odile."

"There's a Saint Odile?" Odile asked.

"Yes, and a Saint Lucy, too."

Brother Bede also had a gift, a hand-carved wooden cross made in the Franciscan house he belonged to, across the river.

"Brother Wilfred made it for you. I have no such skill."

"Thank you so much, Brother Bede. I will hang it over my bed as a blessing."

Naomi gave her a silver cross on a chain. She put it on immediately, intending to wear it forever.

Stewart asked Odile if they should make their announcement, and she said she was hoping to talk to the vicar first about a date.

"I will approach him now," Stewart said and went toward the vicar who was standing by the coffee urn with a scone in his hand. The two men disappeared into the vicar's office while Odile remained to bask in the love of her friends, old and new.

Dear God,

I've been reading the book of saints that Lucy gave me. I got shivers up my spine when I read that St. Odile was born blind and got her sight when she was baptized. That's a message to me, isn't it? I've been blind, and now I will be able to see. Not only that, St. Odile and St. Lucy have a lot in common. Both are patron saints of the blind, and their feast days are both December 13. That's not a coincidence, is it? And December 13 is a Thursday, and Vicar T. said we could get married any Thursday in December or January, in the chapel. What are you up to? Today in my evening prayer you shined a light on the cloud and it looked like moving colors. I thought you were saying the cloud is a veil or a curtain (like the one in the Temple?) that separates us. It's not at all like the curtain in The Wizard of Oz. The man behind that curtain was an impostor. You are the real thing. I'm still banging on the cloud/curtain, but I'm content to know you're on the other side, Lord. Amen.

13
Sex

Odile stood in the kitchen slicing vegatables when the phone rang. Brother Bede grabbed a towel to dry his hands and headed to the lobby.

"2537, Brother Bede speaking," he said. "Yes, please wait a moment. Odile, Vicar Tomlinson for you."

She dried her hands and took the receiver from Bede.

"Hello, Vicar Tomlinson, I'm so glad you called. We'd like to get married on Thursday, December 13---the saints day of Odile and Lucy." Odile listened with a bright face that became cloudy. "Yes, they are both alive. I guess so. Six weeks is not much time. Okay, yes, I will."

Bede had been listening in the lobby.

"He wants you to ask your parents to the wedding, doesn't he? Those parents whose love doesn't count." Though he had come to love Odile in all her blindness and selfishness, Brother Bede retained his rough edges and saw nothing wrong in keeping Odile's flaws before her eyes.

Odile felt ashamed. Her attitudes toward love had changed so much in the past weeks, but she had forgotten her parents in the rush of getting baptized and engaged to Stewart.

"He says I should call them, so they will have time to book a flight. Letters take so long."

"Of course you should call them. You will need to go to a phone box and dial the operator. Take a lot of shillings to pay with. And don't forget the time difference---we are eight hours ahead of them in California."

"Okay. May I call Stewart first?"

"Of course. Your veg will wait."

Odile dialed Stewart's number, and he picked up after five of those loud, insistent rings. He had been up on a ladder, painting the ceiling of the lounge.

"4959," he said.

"Stewart, I just talked to Vicar T. I told him we want to get married on December 13, and he said that's fine. He also reminded me that I should invite my parents. I need to call them. Bede said to use a phone box."

"Bede doesn't want the priory billed for a trans-Atlantic call. You could do that, or come over here and use my phone. I don't mind paying for that call. It's an important one."

"Thanks, Stewart. Will you be home all day?"

"Yes, day off. Painting all day. I'd love to see you. I'll feed you dinner, if you like spaghetti bolognese."

"Not sure what that is, but I love spaghetti. I'll get a bottle of wine and be over after I finish the vegetables here and do my shift at St. Swithin's." Stewart took the receiver away from his mouth as a coughing fit racked his body. "Are you all right?" Odile asked. "Stewart?"

After several uncomfortable moments he came back on and in a ragged voice said, "Fine. See you then," and rang off. Odile hated to start off their marriage as a nagging wife, but she was going to urge him to go to the doctor about that cough.

When she returned to the kitchen, Bede said, "Before you head out for the creche cafe, a letter came for you. It's on the tray in the hall. Your parents, I think."

"Oh, great. Just what I need."

"Now, now, my spoiled American. Charity."

"Yes. Sorry."

Odile retrieved the airmail letter and shoved it into her raincoat pocket as she left for the play group. Maybe she would read it at Stewart's before calling home.

———————● ●━━━

She heard Stewart coughing in the lounge as she came through the front gate to the door. He looked haggard when he opened to her. She kissed him and held up the wine bottle cheerfully.

"Can we have some of this now?" she asked. "I have to read my mother's letter before I call home, and I dread it."

"Of course. I'll pour."

"It's supposed to explain why we stopped going to church. Can't wait to hear what lame excuse she comes up with," Odile said, tearing open the envelope. When Stewart returned with the two glasses of red, Odile had her hand to her mouth, riveted to the letter.

"Must be good," he said, sitting down by her.

"It's horrible," she said. "No wonder they left."

Stewart waited for her to elaborate. Eventually, she put the letter down and took a drink of the wine.

"The church we went to had a large Sunday school. The teacher and her husband were selling kiddy porn on the side, using the children from the church. They used to sneak the kids off to play naked Adam and Eve in one of the classrooms, and the husband would photograph them."

"S'truth!"

"My mom says that was bad enough, but the pastor covered it up when he learned of it. Tried to say the kids were making it up. What children would make up something like that? And now that she tells me this, I think I have a memory of being photographed. I thought it was weird to take my clothes off at church, but I was only about three or four. Oh, my God, the way I talked to my poor mother on the phone! I've got to call her."

"Sure. The phone is in the kitchen. Let's see, it should be about nine a.m. over there, not too early to call. Do you want me to talk to the operator for you?"

"Would you? I still have trouble understanding some English accents."

"Let me have the number," and Odile handed him a small address book from her purse, opened to the Travers page. She didn't really listen to what Stewart said to the operator. He handed her the receiver.

"It's ringing."

Heart pounding, Odile spoke first to her father then to her mother.

"Mom, I just got your letter today. Please forgive me for speaking to you the way I did. I had no idea what you went through back then. I even remember being photographed by that man, now that you mention it. I'm so sorry."

"We were just trying to protect you. It's what parents do. Of course I forgive you. Maybe we should have told you the whole story when you were old enough, but we didn't want to talk about it."

"I understand. Mom, I'm calling for another reason, too. I'm getting married! To a wonderful man named Stewart Fraser. And I would be honored if you could come to my wedding. Yes, on a Thursday in the little chapel. Only about half a dozen people will be there, and then we will go to breakfast at the hotel."

Stewart could hear Odile's mother's voice through the receiver. She sounded excited. The father's voice sounded less so, but not angry. He dared to breathe.

"Okay. Yes, you can leave a message at the priory or at Stewart's. Here are the numbers..." After a few more sentences of love and kindness, her mother hung up. "Well, that's done."

"They didn't sound too upset. I gather they are coming."

"Yes, they surprised me with how well they took it. My mom even sounded thrilled at the end. They'll call when they have a flight booked. I think I need some more wine."

Stewart laughed and picked up the bottle.

"You've earned it, my love." Odile learned that bolognese is a meat and tomato sauce, just like her mother always made when she was growing up, but she never called it that---just 'spaghetti.' They ate in the kitchen and drank the whole bottle of wine, toasting to their love and good fortune. Stewart stepped outside to have a cigarette, but a coughing fit cut his smoke short.

"Stewart, you really should go to the doctor. That cough doesn't sound good."

"We both need to go to the doctor for blood tests before we can get a marriage license. I'll have him check me over then."

"Okay. Can I go with you? What will it cost me?"

"As far as I know, visitors are covered under the national health, so nothing. We could go tomorrow. Surgery hours begin at 9:30."

"Surgery?"

"I think you would say office hours or clinic hours."

"I have lecture tomorrow till eleven. Will you pick me up at Trinity Hall?"

"Yes. Now I have another question. Would you like to stay the night?"

Odile felt a surge of desire in the depths of her body. Yes, she would love to be with Stewart all night. She also felt a surge of fear. "I would. I'm afraid."

"Of me?"

"Of sex."

"Give me a chance to ease those fears. What happened to you five years ago was not sex. It was a power trip, so far from love there is no comparison."

Her heart pounding, she heard the murmur of voices: 'slut, whore.'

"In the name of Jesus Christ, begone!" she said. She looked at Stewart's fallen face. "Talking to the lizards, not you." Then she said, "Yes, let's try."

Leaving the dishes and pots in the sink, they went upstairs to the back bedroom, the one with the view of countryside, and lay on Stewart's bed. They both trembled with the electricity of it. His shaky hands helped her undo her blouse. He kissed her deeply, and she felt the aliveness of her body responding to his. She thought 'surrender' and took a deep breath. Soon, she wanted to feel him within her, but he was holding back, being gentle. She said, "Yes" in his ear, and he entered her. It hurt, but it also pleased her in a strange way. Amazed at what her body did on its own, without her conscious effort, she glimpsed another side of herself, another side of life she had never known. When she arrived at orgasm, she knew the feeling. She had felt it before, though she had no idea when. She had touched her own body as a girl growing up, but she had not felt this explosion of pleasure. This was another world. This was primal. She felt the joy of every woman who has ever been loved on planet earth, a joy planted in her by the universal lover.

When Stewart lay by her side, holding her, she felt the glow that lovers feel after making love. Those lines from 'The Song of Solomon' echoed in her head, and they made perfect sense. You can't understand poetry until you have experienced the feeling yourself. You can't understand God until you have encountered him personally. Odile felt that she had encountered a sacred blessing tonight. She was elated.

"I think I want to go home, though, my love. I don't want to explain to Lucy why I didn't come home. She will worry, and you know Bede won't let me off easy if he finds out."

Stewart smiled. "Whatever you want. Maybe we should wait to spend the whole night until after we're married. Give us something to look forward to."

"Yes," Odile said, glad that Stewart understood. She had no feeling that God disapproved of their lovemaking; in fact, she felt the Holy Spirit's hand in it, but she wanted to keep it sacred and special.

When Stewart dropped her off at the priory, their kiss was the kiss of lovers who know each other as two halves of one body, not two separate bodies. She floated into the stone building as if she had wings.

14
Surgery

At the doctor's surgery, the receptionist called, "Number 47, the doctor will see you now," and Stewart went through the door to the examining room. He and Odile had already seen the nurse who took their blood and asked them health questions for the marriage license application. It would take several days for the test results to come back from the laboratory; then they would have to go to the Registry Office to sign papers and get the license. With all this rigmarole just to get married, Odile was glad they chose a date six weeks from now. Odile looked over several magazines, *Life*, *Queen*, and *House and Garden* while she waited. An hour had passed, and she started to worry. In her mind she said, 'no, lizards, get away, in the name of Jesus!'

When Stewart emerged, he looked pale.

"He took a chest x-ray. He didn't like the sound of my cough. He'll call me when the plates are developed. We can go home."

The lovers spent a quiet afternoon peeling masking tape from the lounge windows to keep their minds off the x-ray. The lounge glowed a warm cream color that went well with the busy pattern of the fitted carpet. Stewart had washed the net curtains from the lounge and the kitchen, and Odile helped him re-hang them. The front room looked like a different place: bright, clean, and welcoming. It was suitable to receive a bride being carried over the threshold.

Dear God,

So much is happening, and I feel your presence at my back through all of it.

I am holding my breath again---worried about the chest x-ray. There's nothing my worry can do to improve or worsen the facts, so I should just surrender again to the reality: Stewart is not well. But you and I together can get him well, can't we, Lord?

When Vicar T. urged me to call my parents, you know I hesitated. I have tried my whole life to please them, and I never have. I guess I thought I could just disappear to England, get married, have a family, and never have to see them again. Never have to see my mother set her jaw in disapproval like she does. But knowing the story of the evil Sunday school changed things. God, why must people mess up the church? Anyway, thanks for supporting me on the phone. It was all right. I was amazed that I didn't get a lecture of some sort. Lord, please continue to stay by my side, and make the x-ray clear. Amen.

While Odile was putting bread dough into the loaf pans, a timid knock came at the open door of the priory kitchen. It was Stewart, and he looked stricken.

"Greetings, young man," called Brother Bede from the kitchen sink. "Taking our Odile on a date?"

"Not exactly. I got a call from the doctor, and he wants to see me. I wondered if Odile would come with me."

"Now?" asked Odile, looking at her flour-covered hands.

"Yes," Bede said. "Now is fine. I will finish the bread. Go ahead." So Odile washed her hands, untied her apron, and hung it on the row of hooks by the kitchen door. She and Stewart drove silently to the clinic, both too preoccupied with their thoughts to make small talk, and large talk seemed pointless until they heard the doctor's diagnosis.

"Come in, Stewart. Is this your fiancée?"

"Yes, this is Odile." The doctor shook Odile's hand, and she noticed his hand was cold. After they were all seated around his desk, the doctor took a deep breath and began,

"Stewart, the x-ray shows a large mass on your right lung and a smaller mass on your left. My diagnosis is that you have advanced lung cancer. Do you want to see the x-rays?"

Odile and Stewart looked at each other. Yes, they wanted to see the proof of the outrageous things the doctor was saying. Afterward, when the images never left their memories, they had second thoughts, too late. The doctor clipped the films to a light box attached to the wall, and the shadowy, eerie pictures jumped to life and signaled death.

"Do you want me to explain anything on the x-rays?"

"Not now. It's pretty clear," Stewart said. "How long do I have?" And Odile let out a sob that surprised her. She prided herself on her stoicism in the face of bad news. Stewart put his arm around her shoulders, giving her part of his strength. She was comforted but ashamed; after all, he would need all his strength to fight this thing.

"Well, you should know that when doctors give estimates of a disease's progress, half of them are wrong, so I don't want to say. As advanced as your tumors are, with no treatment, we usually say six months. But you are young, Stewart, and otherwise healthy. We can do surgery and remove the mass from the right lung. We can give you radiographic treatment. I don't want to give you chemotherapy, though I will if you insist. The chemicals have so many side effects, your remaining life will be full of suffering, and you may still have only six months."

"I am supposed to get married in six weeks."

"Yes, and that is something you and Odile will have to work out."

"Could I postpone the surgery till after the wedding?"

"With no treatment, you have six months. If you opt for surgery, you should do it as soon as possible. Maybe postpone the wedding?" Odile's face fell. "Or move it up?"

"But what can I do for him in the meantime, to improve his chances? Diet? Exercise?"

"First job is to stop smoking. Period. And since you work in a smoky environment, you must quit your job. I will put you on medical work leave, and you will get checks, though small, from the council, to pay your bills. If you find another job, a healthful one, you may work and come off the disability checks, but your energy level will diminish over the next few months. You may not be strong enough to work. I'm sorry. I will let you have a few days to talk over your options. Please call me with your decision so we can schedule the surgery, if you choose."

Stewart and Odile walked hand-in-hand from the surgery in stunned silence. Odile could not feel God at her shoulder.

"I need a drink," Stewart said, and steered Odile into the nearest pub. It had a small back garden with tables and benches, so they had privacy and fresh air to breathe.

As they took their drinks to a table and sat across from each other, Stewart said, "I only see one option. We can't marry. It wouldn't be fair to you."

"What in God's name are you talking about? Of course we will marry. The only question is when. If I can only be your wife for six months, at least we can love for that long. You can't get rid of me that easy," and Odile managed a weak smile.

Tears swam in Stewart's eyes. "It wasn't supposed to be like this. I'm so sorry, Odile."

"Don't be sorry. This is a challenge we can face together and overcome. Think how proud we will be when we show that doctor we can beat his old lung cancer. Just watch us." Her sad bravado touched Stewart, and he kissed her.

"Well, maybe you should sleep on your decision. Maybe ask God what he thinks. Or Bede. Or Lucy. What sort of man straps his bride with a dying groom? I can't bear to think of it."

"No, don't think of it. It's not gonna happen. Let's talk about the wedding. Should we move it up?"

"What advantage would that be?"

"Well, at least in the States, some hospitals are strict about who can visit patients. Wives can, but girlfriends can't. It might give me more power to get past the evil hospital guards. On the other hand, I see no reason to postpone it. Either move it up or leave it on the day we picked. Besides, my folks may have already bought their airline tickets for December."

"Your parents! Oh, my God. What will they think about your marrying a dying man?"

Odile paused, ran some imaginary dialogues through her head, and heard herself say, "I don't think I'll tell them. Until after." Stewart stared at her, scandalized.

"But they are your parents. Why would you keep it a secret?"

"You don't know my parents. If you think I have control issues, my mother is the master of control. I don't want to have that discussion with her. She'll try to manipulate me into doing what she wants me to do. She's done it all my life. She'll split us up, Stewart, and I won't let her have the leverage to do that."

"My sweet love, I think you have a couple questions to pray about tonight. Both of them are serious, in my mind. In fact, I will even take a stab at praying for you tonight myself. I'm pretty rusty, but I think I'm going to need my prayer muscles in shape for the next few months. I'll pray for discernment for you, and you pray for me, please?"

"I will do nothing but pray for you for the rest of my life. Do you want me to come over and stay with you tonight?"

"We promised not to do that. I think we both need time alone tonight, to digest all this news."

"Will you call the Town and Gown when you get home and tell them?"

"I think I'll just say I'm sick, then tomorrow I'll go in and tell Jonathan the proprietor the whole story."

"Do you want me to come with you?"

"I think I can do that on my own, my little Florence Nightingale."

Dear God,

Help me! Help Stewart! Where are you? What are you doing? Why have you forsaken us? You sent me this wonderful man, you made me fertile, we made love, and now he is dying? I thought you loved me. Are you jealous of Stewart? And I don't have any sense that you are there any more. Are you laughing at me? The lizards are making me say all this, but I can't chase them off this time.

Psalm 22, here you go, God:

My God, my God, why have you forsaken me?

Why are you so far from helping me, from the words of my groaning?

O my God, I cry by day, but you do not answer; and by night, but find no rest....

Do not be far from me
for trouble is near,
and there is no one to help. Amen!

At about three a.m., Odile cried out in her sleep and woke Sister Lucy.

Lucy came to her bed and whispered, "Odile, are you all right?"

Odile sat up. "I guess I was having a dream--- nightmare rather. I have nothing but lizard voices in my head, Lucy. Stewart has cancer."

Sister Lucy made the sign of the cross and whispered a prayer under her breath. She sat on Odile's bed and wrapped her in warm arms while Odile sobbed.

"I prayed to God. I prayed to Saint Lucy and Saint Odile. Nothing. I don't know what to do. Stewart says we should cancel the wedding."

"What does your heart say?"

"My heart says...I want Stewart. I want to marry him, even if it lasts six months. I want to take care of him, ease his pain. I want him to have someone always at his bed side when he opens his eyes. One time, we both said we wanted to be less selfish, to do something for another. Here's my chance to do something for another, to not think of myself."

"And you think God is not communicating with you? Sounds like gospel to me. My rule of thumb is always, 'Follow the Love'---ask yourself where the love is flowing and go there. Let me pray with you. Then you get some sleep and tell Stewart just what you told me, tomorrow when you see him." And Sister Lucy took both of Odile's hands, bowed her head and prayed, "Dear God, Creator and Sustainer of the universe, we bless you for your gifts of love and healing. Look with compassion on your children Stewart and Odile. Strengthen them to do your will in the face of these medical hardships, and reassure them of your love and presence. In the name of your son our savior Jesus Christ we pray. Amen." And Odile added her Amen. Somehow Lucy's prayer had changed the atmosphere in the room, and Odile settled down to sleep, feeling safe and at peace.

15
Contingencies

At the Creche Cafe the next day, Odile could think of nothing but Stewart. She went through the motions of helping the children, but her heart was absent.

Alexander came up to her and tapped her on the leg. "Miss Deal, are you sad today?"

"Oh, hello Alexander. I am a little sad, but that's okay. You can cheer me up by playing with me. What do you want to play?"

"Let's play cars. I get the red one," and he sped to the toy box to get the red car. Odile followed, settling for the yellow car and helping set up the wooden race track so they could race. When she looked at the pure innocence and beauty of little Alexander, her thoughts fell into darkness---here is someone's beloved son; what if in twenty years he is to die of cancer? His parents don't know. They will go on acting normal, raising him, when in the end it will be futile. I don't understand, God. Then some lizard voices started:

'Why don't you just leave? This isn't doing you any good. They don't need you here. Go shopping for a wedding dress. This is stupid.'

Odile stopped, shook off her reverie and looked around the room. Beautiful little humans, made in the image of God, surrounded her. Life surrounded her. Love was rampant in the room. God was here, and he had driven out the lizards again. She took a deep breath, and focused on the angelic face of Alexander. 'Follow the Love,' Lucy had said.

Odile smiled and said, "Let's race again. Yellow will win this time."

"No, Miss Deal, red will win!" Alexander shouted. Odile's heart stayed with the children until her shift ended. She donned her raincoat and walked to Stewart's house.

When Stewart opened the door, Odile went straight into his arms.

"Come in, Miss Nightingale. Have a seat, and I will give you the latest news." They sat together on the settee, their arms touching. "First, I went to see Jonathan at the pub and told him. He was racking his brain trying to invent a job for me that would keep me out of the smoke. Capital bloke. But I told him what the doctor said about my getting weaker, so we agreed that I should quit. Then I called the doctor and told him I want to do the surgery as soon as possible, so that I can be recovered by the wedding. He called me back later, and it is set for November 20 at Addenbrooke's Hospital. Then I came home and started working in the back bedroom and the bath, getting ready to paint. I want them fit for my bride."

"Then you have changed your mind about canceling the wedding?"

"Did you pray about it?"

"Yes, sort of. Mostly I railed at God for abandoning us. Sister Lucy says her rule of thumb is 'Follow the Love,' and it is obvious that love leads to a wedding, right?"

"Agreed. And I would argue that love leads to telling your parents the truth."

"I'm not so sure about that."

"What are you afraid of?"

"I don't want to fight with them. I don't want them to change my mind with their emotional manipulation."

"If they can so easily change your mind, maybe we shouldn't get married after all."

"Oh, don't say that. You don't know them." He took her hand and patted it.

"All right. Let's change the subject. Your visa. If we marry, you will get a marriage visa and not have to keep your student visa."

"Yes! That will take the pressure off me. I want to be helping you here, after the surgery, not attending lectures I don't even care about. When can I get a marriage visa?"

"There, that brightened you up. I'm not sure. A phone call tomorrow will clear that all up. Now, another topic: getting you a driving license."

"I have a California driver's license. Can't I just use that?"

"Probably you can, temporarily, but eventually you will need an English one. I think we should sign you up for lessons."

"Lessons? I know how to drive already."

"But do you know the rules of the road?"

"Judging by how terrified I was speeding through the hedgerows with Len and Reggie, I don't think I do. For one thing, the road signs are totally illogical to me, especially when you come to a roundabout. We don't even have those in California."

Odile jumped when the phone in the kitchen started its loud ringing. Stewart went to answer it and came back in moments.

"It's your mum. Here's your chance to tell her." Odile looked furious at him and went to the kitchen.

"Hi, Mom...yes, let me get a pencil...okay, shoot....Flight 2143, arriving Heathrow on the 11th, at midnight. Wow, that's pretty awful...yes, train from London doesn't take long...I'm sure you can get a hotel at the airport and make it here before

115

evening on the 12th. Brother Bede says he will have a room for you at the retreat house...okay, I will tell him...We can pick you up at the train station if you call us from London with your arrival time...That sounds great...Mom, something has come up that I need to tell you. Stewart is ill. He is having surgery in a couple weeks, but we are not postponing the wedding... Very...tumor in his lung...yes, and he worked in a smoky bar... no, he had to quit...Mother, yes, I am sure...I want to help him get through it...I love him, Mom, and I want to do this...I'm tired of thinking only of myself...was that necessary?...I'm hanging up now, bye." Stewart had been standing in the kitchen door, listening.

"What did she say that made you hang up?"

"She said, 'well, that's a new twist' when I said I was tired of thinking of myself. She sees me as selfish, when she is the one who taught it to me."

"My dad called that the Blame Game---whose fault is it that I am a screw up?"

"Gee, thanks."

"I mean, naming who is at fault doesn't improve the situation. I am proud of you for telling them the truth, even if it got nasty."

Odile smiled her false smile and said, "What can I cook for our supper?"

"Spaghetti bolognese?" Stewart said.

Patricia Travers became a bitter woman when life didn't give her what she wanted and expected. She married for love and was disappointed to find it didn't pay the bills. She bought a house in a new development in Progress and was unhappy when the neighbors didn't maintain the houses to her high standards, the neighborhood becoming something of a slum. She wanted a full house of loving children who would adore her and was brokenhearted that she was only able to have one child, Odile, who was affectionate until age twelve and became rebellious and critical after that. She had no hobby, no job outside the home, no faith in God, and no hope. Now her only child had informed her that she was marrying a dying man. Patricia's uncle had died of lung cancer, and she knew that very few survived it. She wanted more than that for her daughter. She wanted Odile to have a happy life with children and prosperity. She wanted Odile to have what she didn't. Neither she nor her husband Mike had gone to college. Odile had a degree and was working on a master's. Odile could marry a professional of some sort who would support her better than her father had supported her mother. Now Odile had chosen a dying bartender! Well, at least she would be a young widow and could marry again. Patricia looked mournfully at the phone she had just hung up, and went to tell Mike the bad news.

Dear God,

Psalm 91: "My refuge and my fortress"---Here I am, back at the priory. God, I need a refuge now. I want to hide from cancer, pain, my mother, the lizards---and I need a fortress to protect me from the onslaught that is coming. I hate hospitals. I hate their smell and the feel of suffering that fills the halls. I want to take care of Stewart, but I have never done that before. I'm scared of his blood, his wound, his moans, his bandages. I'm fretting about it, and I know you don't want me to. Please give me strength and a thick skin not to be overcome by messy sights and smells. Don't let me faint or see spots. I need to be strong for him. Make me a tower of strength, Lord, so that I am no longer a victim of my own mind. Be my fortress or make me a fortress. Amen.

16
Cordial

Odile waited all day at the hospital; the surgery took hours. Lucy came by to bring her a cheese and tomato roll and a mint Aero for lunch. Naomi came at tea time with a pork pie and salad. Naomi stayed two hours, sitting with Odile on the bright plastic chairs. When she left, Odile picked up her *Cloud of Unknowing* book and read for a while, but her mind was not able to focus on words. It was on Stewart and how their life would be now.

The surgeon came to the door of the waiting room, still dressed in his scrub suit and hair cover. Reading his face, Odile took heart.

He smiled at her and said, "Mrs. Fraser?" She nodded; she and Stewart had agreed to tell a little lie to get her access to his hospital room. "We found one lobe of the right lung completely involved in the tumor, so we removed that lobe. The other lobes look clear. There is a smaller tumor on the left lung, but we will leave that for now and shoot it with

119

radioactive waves to reduce it. If necessary, we will go in for that one, but for Stewart's sake we only want to do one side at a time. He is sleeping under sedation in room 339. We will keep him here at least a week, so we can monitor his recovery, then we will let you take him home. Do you have any questions?"

"Will he be recovered by December 13?"

"Maybe, why do you ask?"

"We have guests coming to visit for the holidays."

"I don't advise you to have guests in your home. Stewart will need lots of rest and quiet."

"Oh, right. We can probably put them up with friends. Thank you doctor. May I go to his room?"

"It would be better to go home, sleep, and come back tomorrow."

"You said room 339, right?" The doctor nodded his head wearily, and left.

───────────── ● ─────────────

As they turned the corner into Gretna Gardens, Odile driving Stewart's car for the first time, they saw a paper banner strung across the front room bay window. It said 'Welcome home, Stewart!'

"Oh! Who did that?" Stewart asked, smiling.

"I don't know. Looks like Naomi's handiwork."

"Tell her thanks very much. It's a fine greeting."

As Odile helped him out of the car, Jonathan from the pub drove up. He helped her support Stewart into the house and up the stairs to the back bedroom, which was full of flowers from pub patrons, neighbors, and friends.

"Odile," said Jonathan when she was seeing him out, "My brother is a plumber and decorator. I would like to have him come in and modernize the bathroom. Stew will need an easier-access tub and shower. That old claw-foot is very hard to step into with its high sides, and if Stew is weak at all, he could easily slip."

"That would be wonderful, but I don't know if we can afford it."

"No, it's my gift to Stewart, for all the years he worked for me. I want to do it."

For a moment, Odile felt the urge to refuse. The lizards were telling her 'oh, no, you can't accept CHARITY! How humiliating. Stewart won't allow it. Tell him you can't accept,' but she resisted them. Those were voices of pride, ego, control. 'Yes' is the word of surrender, humility, acceptance.

She said, "Yes, Jonathan, we would be very grateful for your generous gift."

"Right-o. I will call my brother tonight and get back to you soon. Now, another thing: if you apply to the Council, you can get a stair-lift installed for free or reduced cost. You really should do that. Stew is not going to want to be cooped upstairs because he can't negotiate that steep flight."

Odile was grateful to Jonathan for his generosity and advice. She needed help, she had prayed for help, and here was God sending it through Jonathan. As she shut the door behind him, she said, "Thanks, God," and went upstairs where she found Stewart asleep in bed. Leaving him to his rest, she went downstairs and opened the small, under-counter fridge. She found it jam-packed with food. A hand-written note was taped to the freezer door:

'Here is enough food for you and Stewart for two days. After that, Brother Bede will be sending over breakfast and lunch, and Jonathan will be sending dinner. This arrangement will continue until further notice. Call if you have any special needs. To the Glory of God, Fr. Bede OFM'

"Again, thanks, God," Odile breathed and sat down at the kitchen table to cry. How much love exists in the world. How many people want to share and give. She was humbled by their generosity. She herself would never have thought to... maybe she was as selfish as her mother said.

The next three weeks flew by in a whirlwind of activity. Jonathan's brother Will came and tore out the bathroom, replacing the old fixtures with a modern tub-shower combination. He installed rails to grab onto if needed when entering or exiting the bath. A new washstand, tile floor and coat of paint completed the suite. Meanwhile, the Council sent a team to install the stair lift and charged Odile fifty pounds, about a third of what the device and installation were worth. Naomi visited often, bringing everyday needs like toilet paper and milk. She loved to get her hands in the sink and 'wash up,' as she called it. Someone stayed with Stewart each night, sleeping in his parents' room across the landing. It was usually Odile, but Jonathan liked to take a turn now and then. She didn't sleep with Stewart, partly because of their promise, and partly out of fear of bumping his incision. Odile had stopped attending lectures, but was still reading for her two courses, without much attention. She still kept her hours at St. Swithins; she found the energy of the children rejuvenated her for taking care of Stewart.

———————— • ————————

One day, Naomi caught her downstairs in the little-used lounge and asked her, "So, what are you wearing for the wedding?" Odile looked at her dumbly. She had not bought a dress yet. "Right. I will come tomorrow at ten and take you dress shopping in the High Street. Stewart will be fine for a couple hours."

Odile heard the voices urging her to say no, but she said "Yes, that would be lovely, Naomi. Where shall we try?"

"Depends how formal you want it to be."

"Not formal at all. Just nice."

"That'll be easy. Lots of dress shops in the High. See you tomorrow."

Stewart's recovery was progressing well. At his weekly check-up, to which Odile drove him, the doctor removed the last drain tube and re-bandaged the wound. He prescribed rest and good food, and some fresh air and sunshine if Stewart could manage it. Stewart spent most of the day sleeping. When he was awake, he read books. The only television was down in the lounge, and he wasn't bothered about watching it. He did ride the stair lift down and up when he went to eat in the kitchen. Odile liked bringing him meals in his room, but he felt stronger and insisted on coming down for them. It was a good sign. If the day were fine, Odile would set up the garden table on the lawn and serve lunch or tea outdoors, wrapping him in layers of cardigans and blankets. Stewart felt almost well when they ate in the garden.

Odile borrowed Stewart's car on the 12th and went by herself to pick up her parents at the train station. She parked the car and paid for a platform ticket so she could be on the platform when they stepped off the train from London. They would be jet-lagged, she was sure. As she sat on a bench awaiting the train, she talked to God, chatting as Brother Lawrence advised. When she expressed her fears about meeting her parents, she heard in her imagination God saying, 'Come, now, Odile. You have grown a lot in the last few weeks. Don't hold your love back. Surrender it to your parents. I give you an endless supply; you won't run out of it. No matter the response you get, shower them with love. Do it, Odile.'

Just then, the train arrived at platform two, and she watched her folks step down from the carriage, looking awkward and concerned for their baggage. Odile walked up to them with her arms open.

"Mom, Dad, welcome to Cambridge," and she enfolded her mother in her arms and held on. Her mother held on, too. Then Odile felt her mother's body shaking with sobs.

"Oh, my dear girl. My dear girl." Her father patted his wife on the back, comforting her and also wanting to get in on the emotional greeting.

"I am so happy to see you, to be here."

Odile smiled at her, then turned to her father.

"You, too, Daddy. Welcome!" and she kissed his cheek. "Let me help you with your bags," and she picked up her mother's heavy suitcase while her mother managed several shopping bags containing wrapped gifts. "The car is right through here. I thought I would give you a little tour of town before I take you to the priory. I want to show you the church, the hotel, and the cafe where I volunteer with the children."

"Wonderful," said her mother who gazed enthralled at the beauty of the colleges and the churches that studded the university town. "Look, Mike! Look how beautiful!" Odile had seldom seen her mother so enthusiastic. She thanked God for his advice: shower them with love and watch what happens.

By the time they got to the retreat house, delicious dinner smells were issuing from the kitchen. Odile took her parents to their room, a little further down the corridor from Sister Lucy's. All the beds were singles, as the room was meant for pilgrims or families. Her mother chose the one by the window with the view of the cloister garden. The next morning she looked out on the green lawn and the few flowers still hanging on in December, enchanted. But for now, the sun was set and she saw her own reflection in the mullions.

"The WC is just next door, if you want to visit it before dinner," Odile said. Her mother smiled at her daughter's thoughtfulness. Then they went down to the refectory and took seats at one of the long tables. "All the guests eat family style at dinner. It gives you a chance to meet some interesting people." Odile saw Brother Bede wheeling in the cart with the food and got up to help him. Since Stewart's illness, Bede had been short-handed in the kitchen without Odile.

Wednesday night was steak and kidney pie, mashed potatoes, sprouts (which Odile's mother called Brussels sprouts), and apple crumble for afters (which Odile's mother called dessert). They enjoyed the food and the fun of comparing English and American words, foods, and customs. Mike picked the kidney pieces out of his pie because he never ate organ meats, but he graciously thanked Brother

Bede and said he enjoyed the meal. Odile was proud of her parents' kindness and manners. Why had she dreaded seeing them again?

Sister Lucy arrived late for dinner and sat down with them. They passed her the dishes of what was left. She filled her plate and welcomed Patricia and Mike with her usual animation.

"All set for the wedding tomorrow?" she asked.

"We are letting ourselves be led by Odile, since we are still on LA time and disoriented. We are going with the flow, as they say," and Patricia laughed a small laugh.

"Good plan. We will take very good care of you. How long can you stay after the wedding?" This was a question Odile had neglected or feared to ask.

"Well, we paid extra for open-ended tickets. We can fly home any time after seven days. Odile's dad is using his vacation time."

"Wonderful," Sister Lucy said. "There's plenty to see here in Cambridge, or you can venture further afield to see more English countryside, or London." Lucy felt a tense moment at the table and added, "No need to decide right now."

"No, we will see how things go."

"Mom, Dad, I need to take Stewart's car back to him and check on how he is doing. Will you be all right?"

"Of course, dear. Sister Lucy and Brother Bede will take care of us. Don't stay out too late, though, you need your sleep for the big day." Immediately Patricia regretted sending Odile off with her bossy-mother warning echoing in her ears. Why did she always do that? She guessed it was twenty-five years of habit and hard to break.

When Patricia and Mike were about to retire to their room, Brother Bede came in with a tray, a decanter, and four small glasses.

Lucy said, "Oh, what is Bede bringing us?"

"I thought you would like to be the first to taste the cordial Odile helped me make. This is pomegranate cordial.

Your lovely daughter seeded the whole crop of pomegranates for me, a job I dislike. She has been such a help to me in many ways." During this speech, he poured the four glasses full of the bright red, twinkling liquid. "Shall we drink a toast?"

Mike lifted his glass and said, "To Odile and Stewart."

And Bede added, "May God bless them richly."

"Oh, my, that is delectable!" Patricia said. "I have never tasted pomegranate cordial. My mother made jelly of hers. I think we would have had more fun at holidays with this!" They all laughed, and love flowed around them as they sat together, four people whose lives Odile had touched and who had touched hers. The threads binding them together were invisible to them, yet no less strong for that. They had never met, but they were connected, and God was the orchestrator of the connection.

Mike tried to stifle a yawn, but Bede saw it.

"There, that is the sign I was watching for. Time for world travelers to go to bed. Breakfast is at seven. Even though the wedding will be followed by a so-called breakfast, you need some sustenance to make it through the service. Come down for some egg-and-bacon or some corn flakes before you head over to the church."

"Thank you, Brother Bede," Mike said, shaking his hand, "You are a man after my own heart."

Patricia and Mike hung up their clothes for the wedding to let the wrinkles fall out, and collapsed into their narrow monk-beds where they slept soundly in the silence of medieval stone walls.

17
Wedding

At nine o'clock, the taxi arrived to take the Travers family, including Odile, to the church. Jonathan would drive Stewart there. Naomi met Odile on the church steps and took her into the small room set aside for brides to dress. Odile carried her dress on a hanger and wore her wedding shoes. Luckily, the sun shone, but it was quite cold, and the party bundled up in coats and scarves. While the bride was dressing, Stewart arrived wearing the black suit he had bought for his family's funeral. It was many years out of style, with the wrong width of lapels, but he didn't care. A black suit was a black suit.

He met Odile's parents in the narthex of the church. Smiles, handshakes, and names exchanged. He felt stronger than he had since the surgery. Perhaps it was adrenaline pumping in his veins. Perhaps it was the Holy Spirit; he knew that Odile would give God the credit.

Odile's dress, ankle-length with three tiers of flounces, was embroidered at the high bodice and neck with crewel-work flowers in bright colors. It had a bolero jacket with long ruffled sleeves, also embroidered. When Odile bought the dress, Naomi had lamented that her hair was so short. How could they attach a veil? The shop assistant suggested a pillbox hat with a small veil. Naomi thought it didn't match the dress: a hippie princess wearing Jackie Kennedy's hat! But Odile liked the effect. It made her feel like a queen--- maybe Queen Elizabeth II, or the Queen Mother.

In true Victorian Gothic style, Saint Clement's sported stained glass in pointy arches, lots of memorials along the walls, and a big organ to play the hymns. Thinking it much too big for a tiny wedding, Vicar Tomlinson invited the party to follow him to the chapel that served as a sort of transept for the church. Colored light, dim because of the hour and the season, sifted through the window depicting the Virgin and child. Candles burned on the miniature altar. There were three short pews on each side. Mike and Patricia naturally sat on the left of the aisle, the bride's side. On the right sat Bede and Lucy, and a young mother with a small boy. Later, they learned that Alexander had been thrilled to be invited to 'Miss Deal's' wedding. A few parishioners who had pledged to support Odile in her life in Christ also attended. Vicar Tomlinson had announced Odile's wedding to the congregation the Sunday before and told them Odile hoped some could attend. Three old-age pensioners and some housewives completed the small party.

Following the rubric spelled out in the *Book of Common Prayer*, Vicar Tomlinson said all the wedding words, asked all the questions, and got the positive answers. From there, he moved on to the order for Holy Communion. When it came time for the congregation to receive the bread and wine, Odile, Stewart, Naomi, Alexander, his mother, and the members of the Saint Clement's congregation came forward. Brother Bede, Sister Lucy, Patricia and Mike remained seated in the pews, the only event that took away Odile's joy on her wedding day. Neither Patricia nor Mike had been baptized in any church, and therefore they were not welcome to receive communion in the Church of England. Lucy and Bede had been baptized in the Roman Catholic church and would have been gladly given the body and blood, but their church prohibited them from taking communion in a non-RC church. Odile felt that God probably was shaking his head in disappointment at the walls his people built between themselves. Why did they always insist on excluding others or excluding themselves?

Such a small wedding needed no recessional or receiving line. The bride and groom just turned from the altar to greet their guests. Hugs, kisses, handshakes, and blessings all around. After a word with Stewart, Mike made a general invitation for all the unexpected guests to join the party at the Royal Cambridge Hotel. In the end, two of the OAPs came along, but the others all had obligations and made their excuses. The bride and groom drove the block to the hotel, and the rest walked from the church, since it was a crisp, sunny December morning.

The 'breakfast' was more like lunch, complete with champagne for toasting. Stewart barely sipped his bubbly; he had found that the radiation treatments affected his palate for certain foods and drinks, especially alcohol. He did, however, eat well of the roast, potatoes, broccoli, and spiced apples. The wedding cake had two layers: one fruitcake layer for the English and one white cake layer for the Americans. Between was a filling of orange marmalade, and the white frosting was fluffy and not too sweet. Such an intimate party made for lots of laughter and joy. Odile beamed at Stewart, who rose to make another toast.

"I want to thank all of you who came today to give Odile and me a good, strong send-off into married life. My bride gave me a new lease on life, in many ways, and I thank Mike and Patricia for bringing her into the world. May we all live happily ever after," and he raised his glass. Everyone drank.

At Stewart's last words, Patricia looked at her husband and a stricken look passed between them. Stewart had been holding up pretty well, but Patricia recognized that pallor her uncle had when he was dying of lung cancer. The anger she had felt toward Odile and Stewart for making such a foolish choice had changed to pity and love.

The hotel packed up the leftover food for the newlyweds to take home, and they put it in the boot of their car.

"I think I need to get Stewart home to rest. I will come over tomorrow to see you, okay?"

"Okay, my sweet," and Patricia stopped herself from appending some motherly command like "take good care of him," or "put that food in the fridge as soon as you get home," or "drive carefully; you know they drive on the wrong side." Maybe she was learning.

Brother Bede asked the hotel desk clerk to call a taxi, and the four priory residents rode home together. The sun dipped low in the sky, and clouds threatened. The women both wanted to cry, but pushed the sadness down.

"What shall we do this evening?" Sister Lucy asked.

"We could play Scrabble and drink cordial," Bede offered. "Of course, we would have to agree on British or American spelling."

"We could watch TV," Mike said.

"No, we couldn't," Lucy said. "The priory has no telly. Trying to preserve the silence and peace."

"Well, cordial it is, then," and Mike followed Bede out to the kitchen where he found not only the cordial but a large bottle of brandy. Patricia didn't usually drink brandy, but she made an exception tonight. Her heart was breaking, and she didn't like the feeling. The four sat around the electric fire, warming themselves and their brandy. The night passed in conversation that got more honest as the brandy went down. Lucy and Bede guessed the pain Odile's parents were feeling and stayed with them for support. They all loved Odile.

They all wanted the best for her and thought they foresaw the worst.

18
Feast

Odile drove carefully, put the food in the fridge, and took good care of Stewart as she helped him to the stair lift. Both of them undressed and got into the bed. They held each other and fell asleep almost immediately. When they woke from their nap, it was midnight.

"I feel like a new man," Stewart said, "and I have a naked woman in bed next to me. I think I want to make love to her."

"She thinks so, too," Odile said with a big smile. And the most amazing night of Odile's life began.

Nothing separated or hindered the lovers from enjoying their bodies together. They had all night, they had a marriage license, they had God's blessing and their family's, they were free to be themselves, fully physical and fully in love. Their movements were animal and dancelike, human and playful, graceful and rhythmic, slow and urgent, tumbling and static, breathless and vocal, fluid and explosive. They rested and they resumed. They took pleasure and gave it. They moaned and laughed.

Odile felt that their sacred intimacy involved not just the two of them but a third energy. When this energy appeared, she released what she was clinging to---her reserve, her modesty, her fear of pain---and abandoned herself to her body and its movements. She was not in charge. She was just along for the ride. She wanted to open fully to her lover, even if it hurt. She was willing to suffer pain if it meant his pleasure. She surrendered, and the breath of God sighed in her heart. Human love led her to divine love---the unreserved love of another. This was the Great Wedding Feast, the Great Union God was after.

Her orgasm transfigured her. She knew this was what heaven was going to be like, and she wanted it to last forever. But it ended as soon as she thought, 'Please let this last forever.' It left her thirsty for more. She craved true life, and to create more life. Suddenly, she saw the stained glass of the Virgin and heard the words 'She conceived by the Holy Spirit' and knew that all women conceive by the Holy Spirit, not just Mary. All is God.

Finally, their power spent, their love fulfilled, they slept. Morning dawns late on the 14th of December at that latitude. After their 'long winter's nap' they awoke to snow on the garden below. A fairy land had replaced the real world while they had been making love. Wondrous! And Odile whispered, "Thanks, God" as she looked out the window, kneeling on her pillow, holding the blanket up to her chin.

"Yes, indeed. Thanks, God," Stewart said and gave her a sidelong smile that said he was referring to something other than the snow.

"This will be a treat for my parents. We don't get white Christmases in California."

"Odile, I have a proposal for you. You may not like it since you and your mum have some conflicts, but I would like to ask your family to stay for Christmas."

"Here with us?"

"It's only about ten days from now. Christmas has been a very hard time of the year for me for the last seven years. I'd like to have a family Christmas, not a lonely Christmas. They said they have an open-ended ticket home."

Odile felt the urge to say 'no' stirring up inside. The lizards were saying some nasty things. "If that is what you want, we can do it. I will ask them today when I see them. Do you want to ride over to the priory with me and ask them yourself?"

"Yes, brilliant."

At the priory, Mike and Patricia sat on the same side of one of the long refectory tables so they could look out at the snow. The cold morning sun cast flattering shadows on their faces, and Odile thought they looked like young lovers. They could be sitting at a sidewalk cafe in Paris.

Brother Bede came in from the kitchen with a tea pot, saw Odile and said, "Look who's here: the newlyweds!"

"Oh, wonderful! Come in, have some tea," Patricia said. "Stewart, did you order this snow for us?"

"I certainly did, and I've got another gift, too. We are hoping the two of you will stay through Christmas with us. I've had lonely Christmases for the past seven years, and I would like to have a full house this year. What do you say?"

Patricia and Mike exchanged glances. "Let us talk it over. We hadn't planned to stay that long, but it's very tempting."

"Please say yes," Stewart said.

Brother Bede broke in, "The room you two are in is yours through the end of the year. No other bookings, so you are welcome to stay here."

"One reason we are hesitating," Mike said, "is that you need peace and quiet to recover and rest. The last thing you need is house guests. Not to mention that this is still your honeymoon! You don't want the bride's parents in the next room." Stewart and Mike chuckled.

"Well, talk it over. Wherever you sleep, we would like to be with you for Christmas Eve, Christmas Day, and Boxing Day, at least."

"Thank you, Son, for your hospitality. We are honored," Mike said, and shook Stewart's hand. Stewart pulled Mike into an embrace, and tears pooled in both men's eyes. Mike had never had a son, and calling Stewart 'son' choked him up. No one had called Stewart 'son' since the accident. It was a gift to be a son again.

"If you are done with breakfast, we would like to take you out sightseeing a bit, then to our house for lunch."

"Oh, yes," Patricia said. "Let me go get my purse."

"Will we see you for supper?" Bede asked.

"Yes," Mike said. "We don't want to wear Stewart out."

After a driving tour of the colleges and the surrounding villages, the four returned to the house on Gretna Gardens. They had stopped at an Indian take-away for some curry and nan. Odile set out plates and forks on the kitchen table. Her folks had never eaten Indian food and found it spicy but tasty.

"I'd say it's hotter than Mexican, but it's really good. I love this bread!" Mike said.

Stewart took them on a tour of the house. Odile couldn't believe her mother felt comfortable enough to playfully ask for a ride on the stair lift. She laughed all the way up, and the sound of such girlish fun cheered Stewart. They poked their heads in the front bedroom, and it still had all the marks of being lived in by Stewart's parents. The dusty dresser was cluttered with keys, ticket stubs, and perfume bottles. No one had emptied the room after the deaths; Stewart had just closed the door. The tiny room over the stairwell which belonged to his sister Elsie was in the same state; her toys and girlish collections remained, dusty and untouched. Immediately, Patricia formed a project in her mind---she would spend the next ten days before Christmas cleaning out these rooms. Then she stopped. What did Stewart want? What did Odile want? What, for that matter, did Mike want? She was not the boss here. Maybe she was not the boss anywhere, and this idea sent her into a reverie that kept her quiet for the next hour.

19
Eve

Odile was driving her parents back to the priory when Patricia said to her daughter, "Odile, I am working on changing my attitude. I realize I have been trying to run the show my whole life, and I am sorry. Your dad and I would love to stay as long as we can be of any help to you. Let us serve you. You and Stewart are in charge."

Odile's eyes filled with tears. Luckily, she had just pulled up to the curb by the priory.

"Oh, Mom, I love you." They hugged awkwardly across the car seat. "I am so happy and so afraid. I feel like I am holding back a flood with my tiny will. I would love to have your help, if you can stay a while. Let me talk to Stewart about what he will allow me to do in the house---I really had no idea he had left his parents' belongings in that room. You really can't sleep there the way it is."

"No, I think we should stay here at the retreat house for a while longer. You talk to Stewart. Tell him how you really feel, and see what he says."

"I will. Thanks very much. I'll call you tomorrow."

"We will wait in the lobby," her dad laughed, implying that they would sit by the only telephone.

Stewart gladly agreed that Patricia and Mike would live at the priory and work at Stewart and Odile's for part of the day each day. Patricia and Odile bagged up the clothes in the closet and the ephemera on the dresser. They called for an Oxfam truck to come pick up the bags of clothes and shoes. They took down and disposed of the net curtains which had deteriorated after hanging in the windows for years. Odile put the newer bedding in the washing machine but threw away some old, stained sheets and pillows. Patricia vacuumed the room and the woodwork. Mike took down the fixtures and curtain hardware, in preparation for painting. They would let Stewart and Odile choose the color. In her imagination, Patricia pictured the room painted pink or blue as a nursery for her grandchild, then realized that Stewart might not live long enough for that to happen. Funny how joys were always mixed with pain.

Washing, patching, masking, painting and putting furniture back completed the front bedroom, except for curtains and new bedding. Stewart chose the same warm cream they had used downstairs. A nice neutral, it would work in a guest room or a nursery, Patricia thought, then chastised herself for jumping the gun again. She went with Odile to Woolworth's to pick out curtains and a new duvet and pillows for the bed. She let Odile choose everything, but Patricia paid. "It's your Christmas present," she said. They emptied Elsie's room and cleaned it, but did not redecorate. Until the family grew, it would be a junk room (which Stewart called a lumber room).

Stewart was sitting in the lounge when the three workers came downstairs.

"I can never thank you all enough," he said.

"What can we do tomorrow?" Mike asked.

"I think this room needs decorating for Christmas. There are boxes of decorations in the attic, if you can get them down. I can help with putting them up," Stewart said.

"Great idea. We will work on that tomorrow," Mike said, and followed the women out to the car to go back to the priory.

That evening sitting by the electric fire, Lucy told the Americans of a Christmas dinner held for the poor at St. Swithin's Creche Cafe. Churches and businesses from all over town donated food, and volunteers cooked and served it in the redundant church. Since the pews had been removed, St. Swithin's had a large open space where long tables could be set up to feed the needy of Cambridge.

"That sounds wonderful," Patricia said.

"Can we help?" Mike asked. What was happening to them? Ever since they had set foot in the priory, or maybe before, Odile's parents had been filled with love and the desire to serve others. They hadn't once thought of using their presence in England to see historical sights, to attend plays, to shop for luxury goods. All they wanted was to be with people and help them.

"Yes, we need many hands. It's on Christmas day, starting at two and going until we run out of food or people," Sister Lucy said.

"Do you usually run out of food?" Mike asked.

"No. It's sort of like the loaves and fishes. It never runs out. In fact, the Chinese take-away donates lots of those little paper cartons, and we end up sending leftovers home with the last of the diners. God provides."

Mike took Patricia's hand. "We will be there! Right, Pat?"

"Right! I can't wait. Can I do anything beforehand?"

"Bede is the one to ask. He is in charge of the cooking. He usually makes some food ahead of time, like rolls and potatoes. You might lend him a hand."

"Okay, I'll ask him."

141

Odile was surprised and glad when she heard her parents were helping at the Creche Cafe Christmas. Naomi had already told her about it, saying she would be there most of the day. Stewart and Odile's own Christmas would start with Christmas Eve service, then Christmas morning church. They could have their own dinner either at noon or in the evening, leaving time for Patricia and Mike to do their service to the needy.

Putting up the artificial tree, lights, and ornaments from the boxes in the attic caused pain for Stewart. So many of the ornaments held memories, either because his mother had made them from beads or crochet, or because they were souvenirs from family vacations. His mother always tried to bring home a Christmas ornament, even though the holiday might be taken in summer. Stewart told the story of several of them, and then turned quiet, mulling his own thoughts. With the tree decked and the wreath hung on the front door, Mike and Patricia left the newlyweds together for a quiet evening. Stewart had lost weight, and his energy level seemed to drop accordingly. Looking through all those memories had taken a toll on him. Odile called the priory the next day and asked her parents to take a day off from Gretna Gardens. Stewart needed a day of total quiet. Patricia was happy to oblige. She wanted a day to do some Christmas shopping on her own in the High Street shops. She had noted the blue and white theme in Odile's kitchen and wanted to get her a tea set in a dark blue and white calico pattern she had seen in a shop window. Odile had been serving tea from a chipped old brown tea pot that looked like it had been through the war. A nice new teapot, creamer, and sugar bowl to match the kitchen would be the perfect thing.

Christmas Eve day dawned crisp and clear. Stewart felt strong and came down the stair lift dressed in a good shirt in honor of the day.

"When are the family coming over?" he asked.

"I told them to come for dinner at six. Then we can go to late service at ten."

"Not the early service with the sheep and the wise men? I always get a laugh out of something the kiddies do in the pageant." Odile looked exasperated for a second.

"I guess we could change it. I haven't started the meal yet."

"Yes, please. I don't think I can last till midnight."

"Okay, I will call the priory," and Odile went to the phone in the kitchen. Stewart dropped onto the sofa in the lounge, tired.

Naomi took the parents to church and met Odile and Stewart there. The kiddies dressed as shepherds, wise men, sheep, and the holy family had the whole church beaming. Parents and grandparents looked lovingly on their own children while strangers enjoyed the show with all its charm.

"I have never seen anything cuter than that tiny king whose turban kept falling over his eyes. And that baby sheep could barely walk! I think he should have waited for next Christmas," Stewart said.

"Oh, no," Naomi said as they walked out of the church after the service. "He insisted he had to be in the play with his brother, the big sheep." They all laughed.

After the simple supper Odile prepared, the family plus Naomi were sitting in the lounge when a knock came at the door along with the sound of voices singing carols. Odile opened the door to a mixed group of children and adults in scarves and knit caps, smiling and singing joyfully loud.

Patricia went for her camera, "Oh, I have to get a picture. You all look so festive!"

"Please come in," called Stewart, and the crowd filled the lounge with song and happiness. "Can you do 'Good King Wenceslas'?"

"Of course," the leader with the pitch pipe said, and the singers started a rousing version of the first verse and chorus of Stewart's favorite. They followed it with 'Deck the Halls' and were about to fa-la-la-la-la their way out the door when Naomi jumped up and offered around the cookies she had brought. The plate was empty after all the singers helped themselves, which made Naomi very happy. Stewart had stretched out on the sofa.

"I think maybe we should go now. We need to rest up for tomorrow. Remember, Odile, we are bringing a cold ham from the fancy grocer in the High Street, chutney, and rolls," Patricia said.

"And I am bringing a pie and a tiny Christmas pudding," Naomi said.

"All we need to do is cook the sprouts," Stewart laughed.

"Thank you so much, everyone. See you tomorrow," and Odile's parents left with Naomi.

Not only was Stewart exhausted from the festivities, but Odile didn't feel very well herself. The strain of all the socializing was telling on her. They ascended to their room and were soon asleep on their first Christmas eve together.

20

Gift

Neither of the lovers felt up to attending the Christmas morning service, so they had tea and toast for breakfast. The English like their tea and find Americans' tendency to dip a tea bag in lukewarm water appalling. Americans, on the other hand, like their coffee and are appalled by the English tendency to make instant Nescafe. When Stewart handed Patricia a cup of Nescafe, he could have handed her a dead gopher, she was that put off. So, in addition to the blue calico tea set, Patricia bought a drip coffee maker and some drip-grind coffee as a Christmas present for the newlyweds. That way, at least she would get a good cup of coffee on Christmas day. She was working on being less controlling, but she was still focused on her needs. And she needed coffee.

Odile's parents and Naomi joined the throng of volunteers at the Creche Cafe. Bede held forth in the kitchen, and Sister Lucy ran the dining room, decorating the long tables, putting chairs around them, and coaching the hospitality volunteers on crowd control, welcoming, and clean-up. Since he felt awkward in kitchens, Mike helped Sister Lucy. Patricia went to the kitchen.

"Here I am, Brother Bede. Put me to work!" And that is just what Brother Bede did. She never worked so hard, the time never passed faster, and she never enjoyed herself more. She tended the gravy in the kitchen until time to start serving, then she presided at the serving table, dishing up mashed potatoes and gravy in a line with other volunteers, dipping up veg, turkey, rolls, and Jello salad.

At the end of the table, Naomi served slices of the large sheet cakes donated by the local Tesco. Big urns of tea and coffee gave the needy a hot, bracing drink. Patricia smiled and chatted as she handed the guests' plates along the line. Here were people made in God's image, just like her, whose life circumstances had left them poor. She could easily have been on the other side of the table. She looked in their eyes and saw the glow of humanity in each person. She was nearly overcome by the beauty of it, but she was too busy dipping potatoes and gravy. God had never told her 'feed my sheep' in her ear, but she knew she was doing the right thing. She had never enjoyed a Christmas as much.

At the end of the afternoon, when the stream of guests died down, she and the other volunteers started filling the paper cartons with leftovers and sending each guest home with several cartons.

Lucy said, "The count is 850, more than last year. Praise God."

"Wow! We fed that many? I wouldn't have guessed Cambridge had that many needy," Mike said.

"Neediness is in the eye of the person. We never ask for any kind of proof of income. Jesus didn't. Some people are just lonely with no family to go to. They like the hubbub and all the people---it's festive and it cheers them up. They are needy of company and celebration, maybe not food. We're happy to have them all, poor or not."

"I wonder if we have anything like this at home," Patricia said.

"Of course we do, hun. We just haven't volunteered."

"Well, I will now."

The many volunteers made quick work of cleaning up and taking down the tables and chairs. A separate clean-up crew arrived at the end to do that job. Mike was glad because he was worn out.

"Boy, I'm looking forward to sitting down in Stewart's lounge and taking a load off my feet. Where is Naomi?"

"Here I am," she waved as she approached. "We better get on over to Odile's or they will eat all the sprouts, since the rest of the meal is in my car. Ha-ha!"

When Mike and Patricia arrived with Naomi at Gretna Gardens, they started shouting, "Ho, ho, ho! Santa is here!" as they opened the front gate and came to the door. They brought in bags with food and wrapped boxes with gifts.

"Here's a jug of cordial from Bede and a box of assorted chocolates from Sister Lucy. We are certainly not going hungry today," Mike said, carrying a load of goodies into the house. Patricia piled the gifts by the decorated tree, glowing with lights and warming the room.

"I feel bad that you brought all these gifts. I didn't get you anything," Odile said, near tears.

"You got us a son. That is a gift beyond all others."

"Sure is," Naomi said. "God thought so, too." Odile smiled at her father and her friend.

"Shall we open them now or after we eat?" As Stewart and Patricia were busy setting the table and putting out the food in the kitchen, Odile and her dad said in unison "after we eat," then laughed.

Stewart's kitchen table could barely seat five people, let alone platters and bowls of food. Patricia set the food out on the counter and stove top, asking people to serve themselves buffet-style. The five cozily tucked themselves around the table, and Stewart said the prayer, which pleased Odile very much. He was raised to think the householder should say the blessing, whether he provided the food or not. Everyone said 'Amen,' even Patricia and Mike. In the past, they had said it awkwardly and self-consciously if they happened to be present when grace was said. Today, though, they felt so grateful and blessed that the expression left their lips naturally, with sincerity.

After the meal, the men retired to the lounge, and Stewart took the sofa again. The women made quick work of the dishes with one to wash and two to dry.

Coming down the hall to the lounge, Patricia called, "Now let's open those gifts from Santa."

Patricia handed one box to Stewart and one to Odile.

Stewart said, "Ladies first," so Odile opened the box wrapped in nativity paper with blue ribbon. It was the blue calico tea set.

"Oh, this is so beautiful. Thanks, Mom and Dad."

"I thought it would match your kitchen and replace that old brown pot you've been using." As soon as the words were out of her mouth, Patricia regretted them. They were so bossy and judgmental. She didn't know that the brown tea pot she said looked like it had been through the war actually had been through two wars. It belonged to Stewart's great-grandmother and had served tea to soldiers of World War I and World War II. It was precious to Stewart and would never be replaced. The blue pot would make a colorful addition to the open shelves in the kitchen, but the old tea pot would continue to serve the tea.

Stewart saw what had caused the tension between Odile and her mother. They were too much alike, full of advice and criticism. He defused the moment by opening his box. It was the drip coffee maker and the coffee.

"Ha-ha! Now I can make coffee fit for an American. Thanks, Patricia!" And everyone laughed, though Patricia was feeling ashamed. She always said and did the wrong thing. "Come to the kitchen, mother-in-law, and show me how to use it." He took Patricia by the hand and pulled her down the hallway. She felt a rush of love for her new son; he was so kind and forgiving. She squeezed his hand gratefully. She plugged in the kettle and showed Stewart how to set up the filter and measure the coffee. They set out cups and saucers, milk and sugar. Then they sliced the pie and called everyone into the kitchen. When the others arrived, Stewart poured an ounce of brandy on the pudding and set it alight. They all exclaimed at the sight of the blue flames, and Stewart started them singing 'Deck the Halls.'

Dessert was served and coffee poured.

"Let's eat in the lounge," Stewart said, and they all went back to the front room to enjoy the apple pie and the Christmas pudding.

"So, how's the coffee, everyone?" Mike asked.

"Super," Naomi said. "I need to get one of those pots. No more Nescafe for me."

Odile had taken one taste of her coffee and set it down. It tasted revolting. She normally liked coffee, even Nescafe. The others seemed to be enjoying it, but she could not drink it. She hoped her mother didn't take offense, but it looked like she would say something about Odile's untouched cup.

"Don't you like it, Odile?"

"No, maybe I am just too full. It doesn't appeal to me."

Her mother's eyes got big, and a sly smile grew on her lips. She wanted to burst out with her thoughts, but reconsidered. She had already put her foot in it today. She would speak to Odile later, but she spent the rest of the evening stroking her precious idea and smiling to herself. Later, as they were finding their coats and saying good-nights, Patricia drew her daughter aside.

"My dear, I just wanted to let you know that when I was pregnant with you, my first clue was that I had a sudden aversion to coffee. Couldn't stand the taste, and I had been a coffee lover before I got pregnant."

Odile's heart started pounding, and her face turned red. She was not about to faint, however. She was excited, and she threw her arms around her mother's neck. Tears came into Patricia's eyes as she held her sometime estranged daughter. Her heart swelled with hope.

"I should probably not say anything until I know for sure."

"Right. Keep your secret till you can get to the doctor for verification. Will Stewart be happy?"

"Oh, yes. His goal is to replace the family he lost, by hook or by crook."

"I am so happy for you, Odile. Like you always say, 'thanks, God.'"

"Yes, thanks, God."

"What are you thanking God for this time?" Stewart asked. He had come looking for the women since everyone else was out front, ready to drive away.

"Oh, just the many blessings we have had today," Odile said, and kissed him on the cheek.

Everyone rested on Boxing Day, especially Stewart. Christmas day had taken a lot out of him, and he spent the day in bed, drinking tea and eating pie that Odile brought him. She crawled into bed with him and rested her head on his chest. Luckily, she slept on the side away from the surgery site, so she could relax. They slept some, talked some, and Odile read to him from whatever book he was currently reading. She loved to read aloud, and she did it well. He enjoyed closing his eyes and letting her voice carry him to the world of the story.

21

Dance

In early afternoon, the phone rang and Odile hurried down to answer it.

"Hi, Odile, I'm calling on behalf of Brother Bede who wants you two to come to dinner at six. He is making his 'speciality,' turkey and leek pie," Patricia said.

"He told me his specialty was shepherd's pie," Odile laughed.

"Well, you know those Franciscans. They are slippery. Can you come?"

"We have been resting all day, so probably. I will check with Stewart. Count on us unless I call you back," and Odile hung up.

The Old Priory Retreat House was full at the Christmas-New Year holiday. Visitors came from all over the world. Brother Bede always threw a Boxing Day feast with leftovers from Christmas, adding special treats he loved to make, like bread-and-butter pudding, onion tarts, and Welsh rarebit. The cordial had been sent off to the bishops or the Franciscan house across the river, so Bede laid on some beer, cider, and lemonade. One of the guests brought out his guitar, and after dinner they sat around the refectory singing carols and traditional songs everyone knew. Guests from other countries sang traditional songs from their homelands. Odile joined in on the chorus of the French song, and Mike sang along on the German song. For an American song, Patricia and Mike sang their duet version of 'Take Me Out to the Ball Game,' and the Brits teased them about having a baseball song. National and language barriers meant nothing in that room that night. They were all members of the human family, made by a loving God who asked them to love each other---and they did. Before retiring to bed, the guests all shook hands, embraced, smiled, and slapped each other on the back. It was a glimpse of the Kingdom of Heaven, right here on earth.

The next morning as soon as the clinic opened, Odile was on the phone down in the kitchen. Stewart was still upstairs resting and reading. There were no doctor appointments open, but she could come in and leave a sample to be tested. The test took a day to give its result, and the doctor would call with the verdict. No need to see the doctor if it was negative.

"Okay," Odile said, "I will be over by noon." She busied herself making Stewart's toast and tea. She needed to go to the market anyway, so she would drop by the clinic then.

The next afternoon, Odile was cleaning the bathroom upstairs when the phone rang. Stewart, resting in the lounge, got up to answer it.

"This is the Trumpington Road Surgery, may I speak to Odile Fraser?"

"Yes, let me get her. Odile, it's for you!" he called up the stairs. Odile flew down and took the receiver from him.

"Yes, this is she. Yes. Really? Yes. Thursday at ten, Doctor Marsh. Okay. I'll be there."

Stewart listened with a furrowed brow. He was the sick one. Odile couldn't be sick, too. It would be too much.

"What's going on?"

"Oh, just a little test I took yesterday. We are going to have a baby."

Stewart took her in his arms, but he was speechless. What was God up to?

"Say something, Stewart. I am very happy. I hoped that you would be."

"I am. There are just so many things to think about."

"There always are when a baby is on the way."

"How long have you known?"

"I found out just now, with you. My mom got suspicious when I didn't like the coffee on Christmas, but I had no proof till now, so I didn't want to say---get our hopes up."

"I need some time to digest this news. I guess I am in shock, a little."

"That's okay. Sit down in the lounge. I'll bring sweet tea. Then I'll call my mother." And Patricia, thrilled beyond measure, jumped up and down in the priory lobby and skipped down the hall to her room to tell Mike. Shattering the peace of the retreat house---it was worth it for such news.

On New Year's day, Odile took her parents to the train station to go home. Joy and sorrow caused tears all around. Patricia promised to come back when the baby was born, to help Odile in the first weeks. Nobody dared think about needing to come back for Stewart's funeral.

After that, Stewart and Odile settled down into a regular routine. In fine weather, Stewart sat in the garden for lunch or reading aloud with Odile. She tried to get him to walk down the road and back every day, and sometimes that meant umbrellas, but in the cold of winter, even bundling him in coats and scarves couldn't keep him warm. He came home shivering with icy hands that had turned blue at the finger tips. It took an hour or more for the color to return, even bundled up in front of the fire.

Odile had a doctor's appointment once a month to check on the baby's progress, and Stewart had regular check-ups, too. They tried to schedule them at the same time, but that didn't always work out, so Odile got to know the route to the clinic by heart, driving there frequently.

The baby's growth progressed according to normal stages. All was good on that front. Stewart, however, was failing. His doctor took a new x-ray and found the left lung's tumor had grown rather than shrinking. The radiation treatments were not helping. Stewart would need another surgery, if he wanted to fight the cancer.

"Of course I want to fight it. I have a wife and child to consider now. When can I have it?"

"Two weeks from now. And I just read an article on some research done in Switzerland about reducing tumors with diet. I want to send home an eating plan for your wife to feed you. It may or may not help, but it's another tool to try."

"Yes, give me anything to try. I hope it doesn't involve eating snails or Marmite. I can't stand those."

The doctor laughed. "No, no Marmite. Just lots of fresh food and no sugar."

"No sugar? You mean I will have to learn to drink my tea with just milk?"

"If it keeps you alive to meet your son or daughter, don't you think it's worth it?"

"Yes, doc. Just taking the mickey. Thanks for your encouragement. I'll follow your orders like a good soldier."

"See that you do. I'll call about your admission to the hospital. Go home now and show your wife your new diet."

Cooking for Stewart took more work than before because Odile needed to prepare fresh vegetables, and that meant going to the greengrocers almost daily. Stewart had not been eating much because he had no appetite, but now he faced his meals with a will and ate some of everything

Odile made for him. He was eating to save his life and the life of his family. When it came time to go in for the second surgery, Stewart had gained a few pounds and felt a return of energy. The doctor was very pleased, hoping it would speed Stewart's recovery.

The left lung has only two lobes, while the right has three. In this surgery, one of the left lung lobes had to be removed, leaving Stewart to function on half of his left lung and two-thirds of his right. He gave thanks to God for building his body with so many back-up systems. He prayed every night with Odile to destroy the cancer and keep his baby safe and healthy.

When Stewart returned home after the surgery and a week in the hospital, the sore place was on his left side, so Odile tried sleeping on the other side of the bed. This felt very awkward for both of them, but she dreaded bumping his incision and causing him pain.

One night, Odile felt a strange sensation and thought it was because she was lying on her left side rather than her right, but she attended to her body and felt it again.

"Oh, Stewart, the baby is moving I think. Put your hand here and wait." Stewart put his hand lightly on Odile's belly.

He started to say "I don't feel anything," but just as he said it, he felt the tiny movement under her flesh. All fathers are happy to feel this motion, but Stewart read a promise from God in the sensation---there will be a baby; there will be life. From that night on, Stewart craved the time he and Odile spent communing with their baby.

After dinner, he would say, "Well, it's not too soon to go to bed, is it?"

Odile laughed. "Used to be when you said that you wanted to have wild sex with me. Now you want to make love to the baby. I'm jealous."

"You get in on the loving, too. I love you both."

"I know. And it's weird, Stewart, the baby seems to save up his moving for bed. He hardly moves at all during the day when I am around here working or going to the market.

It's only when you are there with your hand on my belly. It's like the baby knows you and wants to communicate."

"Thanks, God," Stewart said.

"Yes, thanks, God. Let's go to bed and talk to the baby."

"Right-o!" Each night they talked to the baby with Stewart's hand on Odile until they all three fell asleep.

One night, when the pregnancy had progressed seven months, their nightly talk with the baby took on a new character. Odile felt that another energy had joined them in their conversation. A swirl of holy power flowed out of her, through Stewart's hand, into the room, then back into her. The baby moved in her womb, more than he had done up until that night, as if dancing inside her.

"Stewart, do you feel that?"

"I felt him move."

"No, something more. Do you feel an energy in the room? Outside of our bodies?"

Stewart waited, listening and sensing silently. "Maybe. Not really."

"Well, that's okay. Let's just be quiet some more," and Odile continued to swirl in the dance for a few minutes more. Then it was just the three of them, falling asleep as was their new habit.

Part of Odile's daily practice was to do the Cloud Prayer twice a day, in the morning and in the evening. Stewart slept much of the day, so she had time to sit silently with God. From these sessions in which nothing happened, Odile drew strength and patience to keep up her efforts on Stewart's behalf. She seemed to have endless energy, even though she was also growing a baby in her body. She thanked God for the stamina he gave her.

During one session of Cloud Prayer, she saw the colorful veil illuminated and felt the comforting assurance that God was just on the other side of it. But she also had a message transferred instantly to her imagination: 'I love dancing with you three each night.' From then on, Odile saw the holiness in the nightly conversation with the baby. It was

a dance with the Holy Spirit. The love and energy poured and
poured between the three: God, Stewart, and Odile/baby.
They were a small version of the Trinity in which divine love
pours between Father, Son and Holy Spirit. It had to be a sign
that God was with them, that he was answering their prayers.
She was elated, and she wanted to share her excitement
with Stewart, but he had not felt the sensation. It was a
consolation only she could sense. Teresa of Avila had said
that the spiritual journey is personal, and one cannot drag
another along on the journey. Odile decided she would enjoy
the dance and thank God for it, not bothering Stewart with
some mystical interpretation. He loved their nightly ritual of
talking to the baby. Why tinker with it? Love is love is love.
That is all we need to know.

One day over a healthy breakfast including whole
grains and fruits, with no sugar added to anything, Odile said,
"I think I should give up my hours at St. Swithin's, so I can be
here with you."

"I disagree. You need some kind of outlet to get you
out of this house, to see other people, especially young, alive
ones like the children at the cafe. What would Alexander do
without Miss Deal?"

"But I hate leaving you here alone."

"Nothing is going to happen to me. I am feeling
stronger every day, after the love infusion I get each night
from the baby." He smiled. "You have already stopped your
classes, now that you have a marriage visa, and if you quit the
cafe, you will be stuck here with me all day."

"Well, I was going to talk to you about whether I
should get a paying job, to help out with the bills. Maybe
offer myself as a French teacher, working here in our home.
It wouldn't be much, but it might cover all that fresh veg I'm
feeding you."

"Have you looked into it?"

"Yes, Naomi introduced me to a lady who teaches
Italian from her home, and she says there would be some
takers. I can advertise on the bulletin boards at St. Swithin's,

the library, and at Tesco's. Plus, I could put a sign in the window."

"I have no objection, my love, if you want to do that. But I still think you need the love fix of seeing children once in a while. It's like taking our baby to play group, in utero." He smiled.

"Okay! I'll get right on it." And Odile got some paper and hand-lettered a sign for the window and some smaller ones for bulletin boards. "Maybe Lucy or Bede could mention it at the retreat house. You never know."

Dear God,

I have to thank you for all your blessings. Today I got a call from a lady who is planning a trip to France and wants to brush up her conversational French. She's going to come here after dinner, twice a week, and we're going to talk French. Also, please keep up the Holy Spirit dance with us each night. I can feel your energy infusing me and the baby, and I think that flow is giving Stewart strength, too. If we keep this up, I'm sure we can cure him. You and me, God, working together, so my husband won't die. I look forward to tonight's conversation. Amen.

22

Gone

"Sister Lucy! What a surprise! What are you doing at St. Swithin's?"

"We got a large donation of baby's and children's clothes at the priory. Don't know what they thought we would do with it, lodging mostly elderly guests. So, I thought some of your mothers might be able to use them. Where shall I put them?"

"Oh, wonderful. Here, give them to me; I will ask Naomi. Can you stay a while, maybe have a cup of tea?"

"Yes, a little while."

"I am due for a break. Take a seat in the cafe, and I'll be right with you." Odile took the clothes to Naomi in the sacristy-cum-kitchen, and she was excited to distribute them.

"Odile, don't you want to take some of these infant things?"

"Oh, I don't think I should. They are for the needy mothers."

"Love, I think you are going to be one of those needy mothers yourself."

"Maybe, but there's a doting grandmother in California who would love to provide for this baby. Let the others have first pick." Odile returned to the cafe, taking Sister Lucy a cup of tea.

"I have missed you, Odile, and Bede has missed you, too. It's not the same in his kitchen without you."

"That is very kind of him. I'd love to keep helping him, but I have Stewart to care for, and I'm taking French students now, to earn a little."

"You are? Wonderful! Would you like me to spread the word at college or at the priory?"

"Yes, please, if you would. I can't afford to advertise in the paper, so I'm posting bills on all public boards, and otherwise it's word of mouth."

"Will do, my friend. And how is Stewart feeling?"

"Much better. I'm curing him with the baby's energy."

Sister Lucy looked skeptical. "What do you mean?"

"Every night, we do the Holy Spirit Dance: Stewart puts his hand on my belly and the energy pours from one to the other, like the love in the Holy Trinity. I know it's working because he always feels energized in the morning. I thank God every day for this gift."

"Have you been reading *Interior Castle*?"

"I have been so busy... not lately."

"I think maybe you should get back to it and journal on the ideas that strike you. We could talk about it here on your volunteer days, or you could drop by the priory. Bede would love to see you."

Lucy didn't like the sound of Odile's description of the Holy Spirit Dance, and she would pray for discernment for her friend. Also, she would talk to Bede, the discernment guru.

When the rain stops in England, there are lovely summer days, perfect for tea in the garden. Stewart enjoyed sitting outdoors, sometimes wrapped up, reading his books and waiting for Odile's next arrival to check on him. She often brought a healthy snack, tea, or a bit of news, like a letter from Patricia or Mike. He was such a slug now. All he did was sit. Once in a while, he would go around the borders pulling weeds or trimming the shrubs, but he usually left it only partly done, and Odile had to come out and pick up the trimmings he left. He was feeling weaker and losing mental focus. Sometimes he would wake from a nap in the sun and have no idea where he was. This frightened him, but he didn't tell Odile. She was so sure that her Holy Spirit Dance was curing him, he couldn't bear to disillusion her.

One day, she came home from the market to find him in the lumber room, going through files.

"What are you up to?"

"I'm getting out all the documents you'll need if I die." Odile hated to hear those words. They hit her in the gut like a football tackle. "Here is the deed to the house, my bank book, a life insurance policy my mother took out on me years ago, my birth certificate, death certificates for my family---"

"Please stop, Stewart. We don't need those now. We're going to live for years. You're getting better every day."

"Odile, we can't be stupid about these things. We have to plan. In fact, it would be best to plan my funeral while I'm still well enough, so you won't have to do it in grief."

"No," she said, and ran outside the house to escape what he was trying to make her face. She was sure God was curing him. Why did he have to say these hurtful things? In the back garden, she saw the pulled weeds, shriveling on the lawn and Stewart's book left open, the pages whiffling in the breeze. He had lost his place. And suddenly she was crying.

———————•◖◗•———————

She dropped by the priory one day to see Sister Lucy, and Bede met her at the front door.

"Hello, Brother Bede. Is Sister Lucy here?"

"Out for a bit. Come through to the kitchen. Lucy tells me that you are using some kind of incantation to cure Stewart."

"It's not an incantation. It's a prayer. A dance between me, Stewart, the baby and the Holy Spirit. We do it every night, and it's helping."

"And who initiates this prayer?"

"Well, we do. We lie down, Stewart puts his hand on my belly, and we say 'Come Holy Spirit,' and he comes. It's wonderful. Why do you look annoyed?"

"Do you think you are God, Odile?"

"No, of course not."

"Does Stewart think he is God?"

"No."

"Didn't you tell me once that you were working on being less controlling? Do you see how you are still trying to control things?"

"I'm trying to help my husband; what's wrong with that?"

"Odile, prayer aligns our will with God's. We learn to surrender our own desires to God and let him do his will. Have you considered that Stewart's death might be God's will?"

"No! God is love! Why would he want Stewart to die? He is my husband. He is the baby's father. He is so loved. It makes no sense. I can't surrender to that. Death is evil, and the Holy Spirit is helping me prevent it killing Stewart. I know it."

Bede had seen Odile at her lowest, in the throes of one of her fits, but he had never seen her as blind as she was today. He took her hands in his rough ones and bowed his head over her.

"Almighty God, please lay your healing hand on your daughter Odile and give her peace to carry out your will.

Make clear to her your desires for her life, through Jesus Christ, our Savior. Amen."

Odile let him finish his prayer, but she didn't say "Amen." She rose from her chair, said "Good-bye, Brother Bede," and left the priory, furious and shaken.

———————— • ————————

When Odile came home from St. Swithin's or the market, she never called out to Stewart, in case he was asleep. She would put away the groceries in the fridge or the larder, make him lunch or a snack, and take it up the stairs to him. If he were sleeping, she would leave it on a table by the bed; if he were awake, she would sit with him, chat about her day, and cheer him up. Today, she had left the priory in a state and didn't want to carry her mood home to poison Stewart's day, so she walked to the market and bought a few vegetables and some flowers. She filled a vase at the tap, arranged the flowers, and mounted the stairs to their bedroom. Stewart was asleep, so she left the vase on the table and went back down. She tried to read the *Interior Castle* book, but her anger was still too fresh. She straightened the lounge, prepared the veg for supper, made herself and Stewart a cup of tea, and decided to go upstairs and wake him up.

Entering the room, she went straight to the table to put down the tea tray, but when she looked at Stewart, something was wrong. His body was lying in an unnatural pose, not the way he normally slept. Panic rising in her, she touched his face and felt the rigor of death. Living faces didn't feel like that. Stewart had died while she was out, arguing with Bede. Why did she go there? Why did he waste her time with his foolishness---God wanting Stewart dead. She should have been here with him. He died alone! For no good reason, she had left him alone. She did not know what to do. Should she call 999? Was that right for a dead person? She breathed, "God, help me. I don't know what to do."

Immediately, the phone rang insistently in the kitchen below. She went down to get it, picking up the receiver, putting it to her ear, but saying nothing. She forgot what to say when you answer the phone.

Brother Bede's voice said, "Odile? Are you all right?"

"Bede, he is dead."

Brother Bede sounded calm and unsurprised.

"Make some hot, sweet tea for yourself. I will be there immediately," and he hung up. Odile went mechanically to the kitchen and put the kettle on. She looked around for the tea she had just made and could not remember taking it upstairs. Her senses were numb. She felt stupid, heavy, moving in slow motion, emptying the old brown teapot and putting in the new bags. She poured the boiling water and sat at the kitchen table to wait for the steeping. A knock came at the door, but before she could open it, Brother Bede slowly opened it and crept in, saying, "Odile, it's me, Brother Bede."

"I am just making the tea," she said.

"Well done, you go back to that, and I will go upstairs. I'll be right down." He mounted the stairs swiftly as she returned to the kitchen to pour and sweeten the tea.

"I poured you a cup," she said as he joined her in the kitchen. She sat at the table, bent over her cup, "I don't know what to do."

"I am going to use your phone. Had you and Stewart made any arrangements?"

"No, he wanted me to, but I refused." Odile looked stricken.

"Drink your tea. I will call them." How many people know the undertaker's phone number by heart? Bede did. "They will be here within the hour."

"Why did he have to die while I was out? I feel so guilty."

"That is very common. Those on the verge of death sometimes can't step over the line because they are being held back by their loved ones. Sitting at the bedside keeps the dying here. They will often make the move immediately after their loved ones leave the hospital room. I have seen it happen dozens of times. They can't go if you are with them."

"Then I should have stayed with him and kept him here," Odile said. Bede patted her hand. They sat silently for a few moments.

"Will you come upstairs with me?" Bede asked.

"Okay." And Odile followed Bede up to the room where Stewart's body lay. Odile noticed that Bede had pulled the covers up over Stewart's face, and she could not see him any more. He pulled the bedside chair and the extra chair away from the bed.

"Let's sit here for a bit," he said. "We will just be silent, like you do in your Cloud Prayer, and see if we sense anything."

"Okay." Odile was so stupefied by her shock that she complied. She took three breaths, letting her mind calm. Suddenly, the baby moved strongly in her womb, and she put her hand on her belly. Her eyes were drawn to the corner of the room, up towards the ceiling. Her head tilted in an attitude of listening, then her face relaxed. She remained still for several moments, and a slight smile formed on her lips. Bede heard her breathe, "I will."

Her eyes were bright when she turned to Bede.

He asked, "Did you hear something?"

"Yes, Stewart. How did you know?"

"When I came into the room earlier, I sensed strongly that his spirit was lingering, wanting to talk to you. So I brought you up. Can you tell me what he said?"

"He said he is very happy where he is, but sorry he had to leave me and the baby. He told me not to be afraid of anything, and to name the baby 'God is with us' because he is." She was crying silently as she said this.

"Wonderful. Has he gone?"

"For now. But he said he will watch over me always. I feel so peaceful, Brother Bede."

"I imagine so. We don't get communications like that often, but when we do they usually make us confident and peaceful. And oftentimes, they come right after the person has crossed over into the next life---they still feel connected here and want to say good-bye. Chances are the messages will continue until the baby is born."

"Oh, I hope so. I was worried about the birth, but now I am not afraid."

"And you know the baby will be born. That's another detail Stewart gave away."

"Yes! Thanks, God!"

"Indeed, thanks God."

The doorbell rang below, and Bede met the undertaker at the door with his folding gurney.

"The body is upstairs in the back bedroom, but let me get the widow to come down so you can do your work." Bede brought Odile down to the kitchen where he got the biscuit tin down from the shelf and offered her a biscuit. "Your body could probably use some energy about now."

"Thanks," Odile said, taking a chocolate digestive. "I should probably eat some real food, for the baby's sake."

"Excellent idea. I would be happy to feed you in the refectory, and Sister Lucy would love to have her roommate back, if you don't want to sleep alone here tonight."

"You are an angel, Brother Bede."

"Your faulty theology is showing, I'm afraid. That is impossible. But I accept the compliment. Do you want to pack a bag?"

"Yes, I'll be right back." Odile went upstairs to get a few things for an overnight stay. She wanted to share Stewart's message with Sister Lucy. Driving Bede and herself to the priory in Stewart's car, her heart was sore but whole.

When Lucy came into the refectory for supper, she was surprised to see Odile sitting there with Bede, tucking into the dinner he had set before her.

"Odile! What a nice surprise," Lucy called as she approached. She had not heard of the death and was confused by the odd looks on the faces of her friends.

"Odile is going to stay a few days, if you don't mind sharing your room with her again. Stewart has passed on to his new life."

Sister Lucy silently took Odile's hand and sat down by her.

"Oh, my dear," she said. "Of course you can stay with me. I will help you in any way I can."

"The undertaker has taken his body, and I have called Vicar Tomlinson about a funeral and prayers. Odile has still to make some decisions, but we can help her with those."

"Sister Lucy, I want to tell you about the message I got from Stewart's spirit."

"Sit down and have some supper, Lucy, and Odile will tell you about her reassuring encounter with the spirit world," Bede said, going off to get Lucy a plate.

Later, when the two women were in their beds, they talked like girls at a sleep over, confidentially and openly, in the dark.

"You know, Lucy, the baby used to move mostly when Stewart had his hand on my belly and the Holy Spirit was dancing with us. I wonder if I can recreate that now with Stewart on another plane."

"Odile, I don't think you should put the Holy Spirit to the test like that. You are not the boss of God. He doesn't come at your command, nor will Stewart."

"You sound like Bede. He asked me if I thought I was God."

"I bet he did. He has such a way with words. He was trying to point out that you are still trying to take charge of things. You want to fix things, to make things go your way. It's a hard lesson to learn, and it is basically the whole message Teresa of Avila is expounding in her book—the book I keep asking you to read. She says our biggest task is to know ourselves. And when we know ourselves, we will be humbled by seeing how arrogant we are. We will finally surrender to God's will."

"There's that word again. I don't want to surrender to Stewart's death. I want to keep him with me through the baby's movements and spirit talks with him."

"And what if God does not want that?"

"Why would God not want that?"

"I can't answer that, or any questions about why God does things. He is always working toward increasing love, and usually we have a hard time discerning how any bad thing that happens can increase love. But we just can't see clearly. He sees the big picture; we don't."

"Yes, well, that has never satisfied me. Why did he give us such powerful minds if he did not want us to figure things out? If he did not want us to know?"

"There you go asking 'why' again."

"Yes, I think I have a right to know."

"Do you hear how arrogant that sounds?"

Odile went quiet in her bed.

Lucy said, across the dark room, "If I hurt you, Odile, I am sorry, but you might want to pray for humility and self-knowledge." Odile was still silent. "Good night, then."

"Good night," Odile said, and she lay awake for nearly an hour, thinking about what Lucy had said. The lizard voices were tearing away at the peace Stewart had given her in the back bedroom. They talked of guilt. They talked of fear. They talked of anger. They talked of respect and honor. They talked of pride and foolishness. They talked of suspicion. When she finally slept, she dreamed of looking down into Stewart's grave. She reached out her hands which held a bundled baby and dropped the child into the grave, on top of Stewart. She heard laughter and looked around to see her family and friends, circling the grave, mocking her. When she woke, the pain of the dream remained. She packed her small bag and drove home, without eating breakfast or saying good-bye.

23
Depth

The day was gray, and the house was cold and dark. Odile dropped her bag in the lounge and wandered from room to room, in a daze. The kitchen, usually light and warm, felt gloomy and chilled. She considered putting the kettle on, but her arms had no strength to lift it. Trudging upstairs, she looked into the back bedroom but could not pass the threshold. The front bedroom was colder yet. She went into the tiny room that had belonged to Elsie and switched on the lights. The narrow single bed called to her, so she found some sheets and blankets in the linen cupboard and made up the bed. She brought the small electric heater from the front bedroom into the tiny room, plugged it in, and crawled into the bed where she slept until she feared for the child's welfare and went downstairs to eat something. She heated a can of soup and made a cheese sandwich. She drank a glass of milk and ate two chocolate digestives.

Then she found the Bible in the lounge and took it upstairs where she crawled back into the narrow bed and opened it to the Book of Psalms. She rested the Bible on her belly and tried to read; then she realized that the baby had not moved all day. She set the book aside, put her hand on her belly and said, "Come, Holy Spirit, come!" She waited. She felt nothing. She waited some more. Nothing. In her anger, she picked up her journal and wrote

Dear God,

Are you real? If so, where are you now? Is it just because the voices are so loud that I can't hear you anymore? I go to the Psalms and I turn pages randomly so you can guide me. Here is what I get:

How long, O Lord? Will you forget me forever?
How long will you hide your face from me?
How long must I bear pain in my soul,
and have sorrow in my heart all day long?
How long shall my enemy be exalted over me?

This is me talking. You have been pulling this stuff forever---abandoning your people. Even Jesus used this psalm when you left him hanging:

My God, my God, why have you forsaken me?

Why are you so far from helping me, from the words of my groaning?

Or this one:

As with a deadly wound in my body,
my adversaries taunt me,
while they say to me continually,
"Where is your God?"

These are the things the lizards say, and they make a lot of sense. It hurts me because I thought you were real. I thought you were with me. I thought you were SAVING me from my early unbelief, but now you take Stewart and leave me alone. And you don't care. I either hate you for keeping silent, or I don't believe you exist at all. Either way, I am lost. Yes, I talked to Stewart after he died, but that could have been a hallucina-

tion---just hearing what I wanted to hear. I don't know any-thing any more. I give up.

She went into the death room and picked up the bottle of pain killers from Stewart's bedside table. She poured herself water from the carafe and filled her palm with the pills that would release her from this darkness.

At that moment, the baby kicked inside her. She dropped the pills and put her hand on her womb. The baby kicked again, and again. Odile began to cry. God did hear her, and he had answered. The voices were all lies.

———————————————— • ————————————————

During a tearful telephone conversation with her mother and father, Odile told them of Stewart's death and asked them not to come over for the funeral. Her mother argued strongly, but Odile said she would prefer her mom to visit when the baby came, that she would need her mother's support more then. She said her church friends had arranged everything and her folks should save their money for a later flight. Patricia backed down then cried on Mike's shoulder.

The churchyard at St. Clement's had received the dead for centuries, but no longer buried parishioners due to modern city ordinances, so Stewart was buried at the city cemetery on Newmarket Road. Vicar Tomlinson did the traditional service from the *Book of Common Prayer*, and a smallish group of church members attended. They had not known Stewart well, but they loved Odile and wanted to show their support of her and the baby. Brother Bede invited them all to the priory for a reception where everyone spoke kindly to Odile, and she managed to keep up a stoic mask until they all left. Then she collapsed into Sister Lucy's arms and cried out her grief.

"I'm sorry. I meant to keep it together."

"And where does it say the widow is not allowed to cry at her husband's funeral?" Lucy asked.

Odile smiled a weak smile, and wiped her nose and eyes with the tissue Lucy gave her. "Please forgive me for the other night. I was rude."

"I forgive you. And I love you." They embraced, and Odile returned alone to her cold, dark, empty house. She put on warm pajamas and crawled into the narrow bed in Elsie's room. She liked the feeling of closeness, like a cocoon, keeping her warmly safe and blocking out the world. Exhausted from emotional strain, she slept. She slept around the clock, got up to use the toilet, drank some water, and slept again. This became her pattern. No food passed her lips. No words passed her lips. She was in too deep a darkness to move, to make, to do, to try. She slept.

24
Castle

The person ringing the doorbell wouldn't give up. They rang it a couple times and waited. They rang again and waited. Again, and waited. Knocked on the door instead, and waited. Again and waited. Odile kept thinking---Go away, you idiot. Whatever you want, I don't want you.

Then, faintly through the walls she heard Naomi's voice calling, "Odile, it's me, Naomi. Open the door. I brought you something you will like."

If it was Naomi, Odile would get up. She came downstairs in a nightgown and opened the door.

"Hello, you slugabed. I brought you some cream pastries from Betty's. Let's make a coffee---oh no, you're off coffee. How about tea?" and she bounced down the hall to the kitchen, Odile following. Naomi fluttered at the sink, filling the kettle and getting down cups. Odile was still in the darkness, but she enjoyed watching her friend being lively. The house around her was so dead and cold, she felt that life was over. But here was Naomi, in platform heels and plaid mini-skirt, taking sugar-dusted goodies from a bakery box. "Now I got one chocolate and one plain, not knowing if you are off chocolate, too."

"No, I still like chocolate. Thanks, Naomi."

"So, what have you been doing since the funeral?"

"Sleeping."

"That is no good. You can't do that."

"I can't bring myself to do anything else."

"The children at the Creche miss you. Why not come and see Alexander?"

"I would just cry and fall apart."

"Then you need to take a walk, go to a film, visit a museum, read a book, something!"

"Lucy keeps telling me to read that Teresa of Avila book, but I can't face it."

"Let's read it together. Out loud. We can take turns. It won't hurt me to know about that saint of the church. We can start now; where's the book?"

"In the lounge on the floor, I think." Naomi hopped up and sped to the lounge for the book. She knew better than to take excuses from a depressed person. She had had some success using her bulldozer strategies on her depressive mother over the past 15 years, and she was determined to bring her tactics to bear on Odile.

"Right. Now you listen to me read, and when my voice gives out or I come to a good stopping place, I will hand off to you. Here goes---and Naomi jumped in with both feet to one of the classics of the Christian mystical tradition, not realizing how dense the writing would be. A natural teacher, Naomi stopped every few paragraphs and discussed with Odile what she had just read, partly to see if Odile was listening and partly to clarify the concepts in her own mind. The book went back and forth between the women a few times before hunger made them stop. Naomi was pleased to see that Odile was making an effort to listen.

"Right. That's enough for today. Now you run upstairs and get dressed. We need to feed that baby some healthy food. I will take you to your favorite place, Wimpy's!"

"Please, not Wimpy's. It reminds me of Stewart."

"Did he ever take you to the basement café at Mark's and Spencer?"

"No."

"That's where we will go, then. It's safe and cheap--- boring English food like shepherd's pie and bangers. I'll wait for you in the lounge," and Naomi hustled Odile upstairs. After their meal, Naomi took Odile home and was happy to see that she was more animated and coherent. "Tomorrow, bring the book over to my place. We can read, and my mum will feed you." Odile started to object, but Naomi wouldn't hear it. "I'll be home at 5:30, so come then. Bye." And Naomi was off, leaving Odile smiling on her doorstep in spite of herself.

Like a sleep-walker following the hypnotist's suggestion, Odile bathed, dressed, and was on Naomi's doorstep, book in hand at 5:30 the next day. A plump, rosy middle-aged woman in an apron met her at the door, exclaimed with joy, and drew her into the house.

"I'm still pottering in the kitchen, Odile. Won't you come have a rest in the sitting room, and Naomi should be home shortly."

Funny how Stewart called the room the lounge and Naomi's mom called it the sitting room. Of course, Naomi's house was a detached house, but much the same in age and layout: sitting room in the front, kitchen down the hall. Odile pondered these unimportant details and looked around the room at the floral wallpaper with family pictures hanging on it. There was Naomi, dressed for a school formal, standing with a handsome young man in a tuxedo. Odile was glad not to have to make small talk with Naomi's mother. Just being in a strange house was upsetting her equilibrium.

"Welcome, Odile!" Naomi said, sticking her head into the room. "I am dying of thirst. Would you like an orange squash? Be right back." And Naomi disappeared. When she returned she had a glass of orange drink for Odile and herself. "Mum says dinner in half an hour, so let's read a little before we eat. I think we are on the Second Mansions. Will you read first?"

Odile agreed to read first and was in mid-sentence when Naomi's mom called them to the table. She put the book down and followed Naomi to the dining room, a luxury Stewart's house lacked. Dinner was roast chicken, Yorkshire pudding, potatoes, gravy, and peas. Odile surprised herself by eating a heaping plateful.

"That's what I like to see. A healthy appetite makes a healthy baby. How far along are you, my dear?" asked Naomi's mother.

"Nearly eight months," Odile said.

"Oh, then baby will be born in September. Probably a Virgo, maybe a Libra."

"Mum loves her horoscopes. She will write up a detailed one for the baby when it comes, won't you, Mum?"

"Oh, yes, of course I will. Now, Odile, how about some gooseberry crumble with custard?"

"Yes, please, Mrs. Warden. Sounds wonderful."

"Oh, call me Peg. Mrs. Warden is my mother-in-law. Ha-ha." And she went to serve up the sweet while Naomi cleared the table. Odile felt herself relaxing and starting to enjoy herself, here with a loving mother and daughter around the table. Mr. Warden was working on a job out of town this week, so Peg was glad of the company.

Odile got her hands in the sink first and started the washing up. Her mother always did the same. Patricia had counseled, "Get right in there and start washing. You have no idea where the dishes go in someone else's kitchen, but washing requires no special knowledge." Peg was happy to dry and put away some of the pans and utensils, but she had a clever dish rack over the drain board where the dishes went straight from the sink and were left to dry without further fuss. Odile envied this rack. She could have asked Stewart to build her one, if...

"Now, girls, go on with your reading. I won't bother you except to bring you a cup of tea a little later. I have a telly upstairs I can watch. I can't miss 'Coronation Street'!"

Back in the sitting room, Naomi took the book, saying, "You know I really liked the idea that God has been calling us over and over through sermons and people, and books, and illnesses."

"I always used to cry to God when I was really ill, even though I didn't believe in him. Weird, huh?"

"I think that's what she means. He calls even when we don't believe. How can we be so stupid to keep resisting?"

"I think we listen to the reptiles and believe them, rather than God and his messengers," Odile said.

Naomi resumed reading until she was stopped by a word new to her. "What does 'aridity' mean?"

"Dry like a desert. I guess it means that sometimes in silent prayer nothing happens and it feels dry and dull. I have had that happen. A lot, to be honest."

"But then she says not to lose heart, keep striving to go deeper, to get closer, and even if you fail, God will bring something good out of it."

"Do you believe that, Naomi?"

"Yes, I do. When something goes wrong, you think it is the end of the world, but sometimes it just clears the way for something better. I felt that when I crashed my old Mini. I cried for a week, but then my best friend's dad got a new car and sold me his old one for a quid! And it was years newer than the Mini." She noticed Odile looking skeptical. "Of course, I don't yet see what good will come out of Stewart's death. I'm not trying to say that was a good thing. Not yet, anyway." Naomi went silent, feeling awkward.

"I'll read," Odile said, and started on the Third Mansions, a place of more comfort since the reptiles were not so annoying, but where humility still eludes the person trying to get along on the journey. "I can see how once you start doing charity and leading a good life, you might start to think you are special and deserve more favor from God. You may be doing charity just to make yourself look good."

"And what does God want with your works anyway? All he wants is your surrender. I know you hate that word, but maybe you hate it because you cling to your own power." Naomi looked surprised at her own insight. "Sorry if that sounded bossy."

"I did surrender once. To Stewart, when we were making love. I let go of all my tightness and opened fully."

"What was that like?"

"It was like heaven. It was like being what I was meant to be. Like fitting my skin, finally. I can't describe it."

"I think you just did. And if surrendering to a man you love is like heaven, what must surrendering to God be like?" The young women looked at each other, speechless. They knew they were touching the edge of a great mystery that Teresa of Avila tried to explain centuries ago. The mystery boggled the rational mind, but spoke to the soul in a language it understood. Odile and Naomi, beginners on the journey, were nevertheless wise enough to know they were in the presence of something holy, something ineffable. "Wow," breathed Naomi, and they both laughed, a little joyous and a little uncomfortable.

At the door they heard a spoon being struck melodically on a tea cup.

"Tea time, girls," called Peg as she opened the door and brought in two cups of tea on a tray. "I brought the biscuit tin, too, just in case. All that reading is hard work, you know," and she bustled away.

"Odile," Naomi said, as they drank their tea, "I confess that I started this reading just to get you out of your funk, but I am glad we are reading this. It is having an effect on me. You know that my love for church has always been rather social and traditional. I never thought that much about prayer or trying to be in harmony with God's will. I want to thank you for sharing this book with me. It is a life-changer."

"God calling you through Teresa of Avila."

"Yes, and through Odile Travers."

"And calling me through Naomi Warden."

"Yes."

Then the girls spoke in unison, "Thanks, God!" and laughed, smiling love at each other.

When Naomi arrived at Gretna Gardens, she expected to have to ring, knock, and shout to raise the sleeping Odile, but she was surprised when her friend came promptly to the door, tea towel in hand, busy and smiling.

"Come to the kitchen. I'm just about to put the pasta in the water." They had Odile's spaghetti and salad, followed by ice cream and biscuits. No wine this time, for the baby's sake. Later, in the lounge, they tackled the Fourth Mansions together. This mansion is harder to understand, for it deals with supernatural prayer and God sending consolations to the soul.

"All I got out of that section was 'think less; love more,'" Naomi said. "If that's what God wants, I think I can do that."

"Not me. I am always thinking, planning, worrying."

"Yes, and she says you bring all that stress on yourself because you don't understand yourself."

"What do I need to understand?" Odile asked, frustrated.

"I think she means you need to understand that you have God right there with you, and you need to relax and let it be. Not worry so much. Didn't you say you felt fearless after talking to Stewart's spirit?"

"Yes, but that seems like a dream now, like I was just making it up."

"Did the lizards tell you that?"

"Yes."

"No more lizards allowed in your head, Odile! When they come, you have to ask God to drive them off."

"I hate to bother him for little things like that."

"Well, that is the silliest thing you have said yet. Bother him? Didn't he say you are precious to him? Do you think helping you bothers him? And lizards are not a little thing; they are the henchmen of the devil, your biggest enemy. This is what Teresa means---you don't know yourself, who you are, how loved you are."

"If he loves me so much, why did he take Stewart?" Odile choked.

"I hear an echo of lizard speak in that. Here, hand me the book; I'll read a while," and Naomi took over reading while Odile composed herself. When Naomi was reading about the flow of supernatural water that wells up in the soul directly from God's spring during the Prayer of Quiet, Odile interrupted her.

"That is what it felt like when we did the Holy Spirit dance together. The love and energy just filled me and flowed out into Stewart and around and back into me. We didn't do anything special to get it. Does that mean I have reached the fourth mansion?"

"Maybe, Teresa says all the nuns she is talking to can expect to at least enter that level, but I don't think you should look at it as something to achieve. She tells the nuns not to strive for it because it is prideful to think you can make God do what you want, either by straining or by earning it with good deeds. He gives what he wants when he wants."

"Will you tell me again that part about humility?"

"She says you will know you are humble when you don't feel you deserve the consolations God sends you. Do you feel you deserve them?"

"Not really, but I do strive to get them. I think I can make him answer me, and that is arrogant."

"Let's keep going. You read now," and Naomi handed over the book. Before long, she interrupted Odile's reading. "What do you think she means by detachment?"

"I guess, the willingness to let go of things. Like I was willing to let go of my master's degree after I started doing the Cloud Prayer. It just didn't mean anything to me any more; I preferred to take care of Stewart."

"And I let go of my boyfriend Terry. We had been dating for four years, and he broke it off. I tormented myself for months after that. When I finally let go, all of a sudden I felt free, alive, like a new person. But how far does God want us to take this detachment thing?"

"Detachment from our ego, our self image, our power, our own will. That's what surrender means, I guess. Giving up everything but God. I don't know if I can do it."

"Maybe it's not something you do. God does it. You just allow it." Again, the girls were aware they were skating out on the thin ice of a mystery. Teresa was saying to leave the will in God's hands and let him use it. Raised in human society with an ingrained work ethic and the drive to succeed, both girls couldn't imagine how to do that, but they trusted the author knew best, and kept reading.

One section spoke especially to Odile. Teresa was describing how some people, wandering around with no thought of God find themselves suddenly inside the castle, called by God as a shepherd calls his lost sheep.

"Naomi," Odile interrupted herself, "that is what happened to me! I fell off the punt with no thoughts of God in my head, and God rescued me and set me on this path, in the midst of nuns, friars, Christians, cathedrals, prayer. I was his lost sheep. I wasn't even trying to enter the castle."

"I think you're right. There's more evidence that you're in the fourth mansion. Super. But then she says you should forget about it and spend your time in thanksgiving and worship."

"Not thinking about my pleasure, my comfort, my achievement, or any of that. Being detached."

"From everything but God." Some of it was coming clearer to the girls. As Naomi said good-night and went to her car, she turned to Odile sheepishly and said, "I can't come over to read tomorrow. They've asked me to fill in at work."

"That's okay. I'll keep reading on my own and I'll share it with you next time, whatever I can comprehend. Just call me when you're free. I will be fine. You've helped me a lot, little angel."

They embraced. Think less; love more. They would work on it.

Dear God,

I am reading on my own now, trying to get what Teresa is saying about the Fifth Mansions, and one thing struck me. She says that a soul that has been implanted with you has no doubt that you have been there, and that the certainty is 'material.' I felt your presence in the river when you filled me with air so I could float up, and I felt the flowing of the love as a physical thing during our dance. But then she says that the soul who leaves its silkworm cocoon is not bound by any ties--- not relationships, friendships or property. But I still am bound by those things; I own this house, I love my baby, I am friends with many people. Then she says that your desire is for me to love you and love my neighbor. Well, how can I love my neigh-bor if I cut all ties to them? I am confused. Please help me to understand myself and this book. Amen.

———————— • ————————

Peg Warden picked up the phone in her kitchen, "Hello?"

"Hello, Mrs. Warden, Peg, this is Odile."

"Hello, Odile, dear. Naomi is still at work."

"Oh, I just wanted to tell her that I am taking the book back to Sister Lucy tonight, and we will be having a major discussion about it. If she wants to join us, she would be very welcome. In fact, I hope she will come. If she gets there by six, she can have dinner with us in the refectory."

"That sounds lovely. I will tell her when she gets home."

"Thank you."

"Ta! Bye, Odile," and Peg rang off. Odile wondered why Peg answered her phone with "hello" rather than the phone number. She would never figure out the English.

Dinner in the refectory was a cozy and convivial affair, with a rich and exotic moussaka that Bede was experimenting with. Everyone raved about it and encouraged him to make it again. He was pleased. They all retired to the chairs around the fire before embarking on the *Interior Castle* discussion. They felt that Odile was in a state about it, so they had not brought it up at dinner, not wanting to spoil the fellowship.

"So, Odile, how can we help you with Teresa of Avila?" Sister Lucy asked.

"Frankly, I was about to throw the book out the window, but then I realized that it was not my book. So, I am bringing it back to you with thanks and with a feeling of frustration."

"How far did you get, Odile, after we stopped reading together?" Naomi said.

"I got through the Sixth Mansions, then I gave up. I was finding a few ways I fit level six, but I was sure I am not at level seven, and her writing was leaving me in the dust."

"When we were reading together, lots of the things she talked about left me behind, but you got them," Naomi said. "You are practicing silent prayer, and I am not. I think you can understand her if you have experienced the thing yourself. If you haven't, you can't."

"I agree with Naomi. Maybe you should pick up the book again after a few months or years, further along in your spiritual journey."

"Or maybe Teresa of Avila is only one person telling of her own experience. You need not take her word for gospel. Remember Brother Lawrence told you that silent prayer didn't work for him at all. He preferred talking to God aloud and casually, like a companion, not like some exalted majesty in a crystal palace. I never have liked Teresa's imagery," Brother Bede said.

"Well, I do like the crystal images because I see those myself, but I got excited then angry in the sixth level. When she started talking about locutions, my ears perked up. That's what I have experienced myself," Odile said.

"What are locutions?" Naomi asked.

"When God speaks to you," Bede answered.

"You mean out loud, or just in your imagination?"

"Both. Teresa says there are locutions you can hear with your ear, with your imagination, and with your intellect," Odile said, "and I have had several of them since I have been here."

"How are you supposed to know if they are really from God?" Naomi asked.

"Oh, she's got answers for that, too," Bede huffed. "The woman knows it all."

"She says that they make you peaceful and they stay in the memory a long time. You never forget the words God says to you. And they come when you don't expect them, like when you are scrubbing the floor," Odile smiled at Bede.

"And," Lucy said, "they agree with scripture. I seem to remember that a couple of yours actually came from scripture, and that was before we started our Bible study."

"Yes, 'feed my sheep' and 'arise my love, my fair one, and come away,'" Odile said. "Then she talks about visions, and I think we could count Sister Lucy on the bridge looking like an angel, the spotlight on the potatoes and the word 'control,' and maybe the vision of my parents."

"Definitely the parental vision. That was the result of scrub-therapy, and scrub-therapy always works," Bede laughed.

Lucy said, "So what made you angry about the Sixth Mansions, if you were finding your own experience there?"

"Well, then she went on to talk about being pierced by an arrow and having your guts pulled out and how painful and pleasing that was. And she said you would have raptures where your soul would be carried out of the body and taken by God so he could show you a glimpse of the kingdom, and when you came back to your senses, you would be in a daze for days. I haven't had any of those."

"So basically, you were frustrated that Teresa's description didn't match your experience exactly," Naomi said.

"And you weren't able to pigeon-hole yourself in the Sixth Mansion perfectly," Bede scoffed.

"And you couldn't congratulate yourself on your achievement," Lucy added.

Odile went quiet, crushed by the truth her friends had just confronted her with. Again, she was trying to control, to be perfect, to make Teresa's book fit her own life, and if it didn't it was going out the window. Humility. Self-knowledge. These were Teresa's watch-words. And Odile still didn't have them.

"I believe Teresa says many times that she may be mistaken and that these steps may not fit for everyone, since God can give favors to anyone at any time. God doesn't have to act on Teresa's plan. He does as he likes when he likes," Lucy said.

"Exactly!" Bede burst out. "Controllers are always trying to put God in a box. God is not an object to be analyzed with hierarchies and metaphors. God is God, and that mystery is not for us to know. Just love God and others. That's it. Why make it so complicated?"

"Think less; love more," Naomi said.

"That's the ticket!" Bede laughed, rising to go to the kitchen. "Time for some brandy, I think."

"I have never stopped being an arrogant, self-centered idiot, have I?" Odile said.

"Maybe not, but that is the human condition. We all think of ourselves naturally; we have to learn compassion. Don't be too hard on yourself, Odile. That is the perfectionist lizard talking," Lucy said.

Bede poured the four friends small glasses of brandy. "Shall we drink a toast?"

"To humility," Odile said.

"To self-knowledge," Naomi said.

"To love," Bede said.

And Lucy added, "Amen." They all hoisted their glasses and drank, Odile taking a very small sip, for the sake of the baby. She had a lot to think about, and she was grateful for her friends, for Teresa of Avila, and for God's love. When she got home, she would read her Bible, pray, and sleep in her cocoon bed. Maybe next morning she would emerge a humble butterfly.

25
Emmy

In August, when her teaching fellowship at Jesus College came to an end, Sister Lucy had to return to her Dominican convent in Glasgow. Odile taught French to two adult students and one teenager each week and made her appearance at the Creche Cafe a couple times a week. She cooked at home to save money, but she ate with Bede in the refectory on Sundays. When September rolled around, Odile went to see the doctor weekly, and he assured her that the baby was fine and growing well. She was a little worried because the movements had stopped.

"The baby is too tight in there to move much, now that he's so big. Don't worry about it; the heart beat is strong," the doctor reassured her.

She still prayed silently twice a day, read her Bible, and talked to God casually as she worked around the house. She also talked to the baby, some days calling it 'Manny,' and some days calling it 'Emmy.' Stewart had told her to name the baby 'God is with us,' so she had chosen a female and a male spelling: Emmanuelle and Emmanuel. On the days when the baby was a girl, Odile called her 'Emmy' for short. The boy's nickname was 'Manny.' Her mind and heart focused more and more on the baby as its birth date drew nearer. She found herself in a reverie much of the day, and she was relieved to crawl into her small bed at day's end. The weight of the baby tired her. She even took to riding Stewart's stair lift to go up to bed at night.

Early in the morning of September 17th, Odile turned over in bed and felt a warm gush between her thighs as her water broke. What was she supposed to do? She took a deep breath and said to her companion God, "Are you with me, God? Here we go," and putting a towel from the linen cupboard between her legs, she rode down the stairs to the kitchen where she called Naomi's house. Peg and Naomi had said she could call them at any hour if she needed them.

Naomi picked up, "Hello, is it Odile?"

"Yes, it's me. My water broke."

"I'll be right there. You call the doctor."

"Right." And calmly as she could, she dialed the doctor's number with shaky hands. When Naomi arrived, Odile was dressed and ready. Her bag had been packed weeks ago and placed by the front door. Naomi grabbed it as she helped Odile to the car.

"I've put some extra towels on the car seat, just in case," Naomi said.

"Thanks." And the two young women drove to the hospital emergency entrance where a wheel chair met them and whisked Odile to the maternity ward.

Naomi went home, took a shower, had breakfast, and returned to the hospital waiting room with Peg, who just loved the excitement of waiting at the hospital for a baby to come. She had brought her yarn and crochet hooks; making something for the baby was the perfect pastime, and people in the room might mistake her for a grandmother, which thrilled her no end. Since the Wardens were not family, they were not allowed in the labor room, but they got updates from the nurses, assuring them that things were progressing normally for Odile. The labor was likely to take several hours, since this was her first birth. Naomi phoned Odile's parents from her home phone, letting them know that labor had just begun. Patricia said she would get on the first flight she could book. Naomi promised to call if the baby came. Chances are that Patricia would be in transit and would not get the call, but Mike would. Patricia would check in with him when she landed.

In the labor room, Odile breathed deeply, partly to ease her pains, but also to pull as much of the Holy Spirit into her body as possible. She knew God dwelt within her, but she also knew that God surrounded her on all sides. When the contractions came, she said to herself, 'Don't tighten up. Don't hold your breath. Don't try to stop the pain. Let it be. Let it go.' She knew her love of control had never served her well, and she doubted it would help her give birth to her child. She remembered the night of surrender that had conceived this baby, and she hoped to duplicate the feeling here. When the contractions came they were so strong that she couldn't help clenching against the pain, and she cried out. The nurse kept a hand on her to reassure her and reminded her to breathe. In the minutes between pains, she returned to her prayerful state, breathing deeply of the Holy Spirit. She felt safe and brave, and she thought she could surrender. As the contractions came closer and faster, she could only feel the worst pain she had ever felt, and she thought, 'God, please let me die. It's too much. I want to die.'

At that point, the nurse said, "All right, Odile, you are going to want to push, but don't push yet. We are taking you into delivery. Just breathe. The baby is about to come," and they wheeled Odile into an operating room and lifted her onto the delivery table, wrapped in several sheets, with her heels belted into stirrups. She had never done any of this before. She was lost, stupid, small. She had to let others do for her. She had to listen to instructions. She had to be led.

She had to surrender. Surrender freed her from being right, perfect, and in charge.

Then the nurse said to her, "When you push, it will feel like you are going to poop. Push anyway. Don't hold back," and Odile was not dismayed at the prospect. She would push, no matter how indelicate it felt. She would shed her propriety, her modesty, her squeamishness. None of those were helpful here. Her body had holy work to do, and she would let it work.

When another contraction came, another killer that made her want to die, the nurse told her the optimal moment to push, and Odile obeyed. The push relieved the pain, and she marveled at how God had made her body.

"There's the head. Well done, Odile. A couple more good pushes. Breathe, Odile." Odile focused on the nurse's commands and on her own body. She was not thinking. She was not trying. She was surrendered to the sacred process that had been going on for millennia. She obeyed when the nurse told her to push again, and when she said, "Don't stop. Keep pushing." After that one, Odile felt spent. She rested for the short space before the next contraction. Then the nurse said, "This one might do it." Odile pushed, and the nurse said, "Good girl, Odile, the baby's out."

She looked down over her belly and saw the nurse taking a red, naked doll over to a table.

The doctor stood over her and said, "You have a daughter."

In Odile's imagination she heard Naomi say, 'Think less; love more,' and a flood of love filled her heart---for her daughter, for Naomi, for the nurse, for the doctor, for God, for Stewart, for everyone. She smiled in a reverie of love as she delivered the afterbirth, as she submitted to being cleaned, changed, blanketed, and wheeled into recovery. This might have been one of the raptures Teresa was talking about, but Teresa had never had quite this experience. Think less; love more. Odile felt she was love incarnate, and her body of love had produced another body of love, after union with another body of love. It was all love. It was all God.

Her amazing, strong body had done a miraculous thing, but her legs were shaking and she couldn't stop them. When a nurse came in to check, Odile said, "I can't stop my legs shaking." The nurse brought more blankets and wrapped her tightly, but they kept shaking. She realized she could not control her legs. She panicked for a moment, and then she gave in; she let them shake until they stopped on their own. Then she rested. Soon thereafter, she was taken to a room, put in bed, and brought her baby.

At the waiting room, the nurse stuck her head in to tell Naomi and Peg that the baby was born, and it was a girl. Mother and daughter hugged each other in joy, and Naomi went to the phone kiosk in the hall to call Mike.

"She is in room 315, if you want to see her and the baby," the nurse said, and Peg nearly jumped for joy.

The nurses really preferred that visitors not hold the baby, but Peg could not be stopped, though Naomi said she would wait till the baby was bigger.

"What is this little lamb's name?" Peg asked.

"Her name is Emmanuelle Luce Fraser," Odile said, and at that moment she felt a presence in the room that threw a warm blanket of peace over them all. Her eyes were drawn to the ceiling of the room where she saw but at the same time didn't see a cloudy brightness that she knew to be Stewart's love for her and the baby. No fear, no thoughts, could spoil this miraculous day when the birth of new life united her with her husband again. She looked into Emmy's eyes and saw Stewart's there, and though the baby's hair was sparse and black, she foresaw the red hair her daughter would sport throughout her life, until it grayed in her old age. Not only is God with me, but Stewart will be with me in this little one, Odile thought.

"Thanks, God," she said aloud.

In unison, Peg and Naomi said, "Amen."

26
Reunion

Odile was surprised that English mothers expected to have a week-long hospital stay after giving birth, all at the expense of the National Health Service. Such a luxury was rare in the States, and new mothers were sent home as soon as possible if there were no complications. Odile felt pampered by the nurses who brought her meals and her baby to nurse and hold. Naomi and Peg visited daily and brought flowers and the crocheted cap Peg had whipped up in the waiting room.

"Your mum called us, and we told her where you hid the key to the house so if she arrives late, she can let herself in," Naomi said. "I expect she will come straight here if she arrives in daylight."

"Probably," Odile said.

"Now, Odile, I have a serious subject to bring up," Peg said. Odile and Naomi looked at her doubtfully. "Where are you going to raise your daughter? Here or in the US?"

"I don't know. I love it here."

"Yes, but your parents, the child's grandparents, live in the States."

Naomi added, "Sister Lucy always said, 'Follow the love.'"

"It would be nice to tell your mum when she gets here that you are coming home," Peg said.

Odile hesitated, listening to her heart's voice. Then she said, "You're right. For Emmy's sake and for my parents' I need to go home."

"And I will come visit," Naomi said. "I have always wanted to see California."

———— • • ————

Patricia arrived exhausted in the middle of the night. She had taken a train from Gatwick to London, another train to Cambridge, and a taxi to Odile's house where she found the key under the first brick in the edging of the flower bed. The house was cold, but she made her way upstairs and collapsed in the bed she and Mike had fitted out in the front bedroom. When the sun came in the windows, she bathed, found some tea and bread in the kitchen, ate quickly, and went to the hospital where Odile and her granddaughter waited. It was a joyous meeting of the three generations, made even more joyous by Odile's decision to move back home with Emmanuelle. It would take some time to sell the house, the car, and dispose of a houseful of furniture. Patricia said she would stay as long as necessary to help, and Odile was relieved and grateful. She had never realized her mother's love as clearly as she did now. Love was starting to make more sense to her, the more she herself loved.

During the remaining days of Odile's hospital stay, Patricia got used to driving on the wrong side of the road and found her way to Mothercare and Boots and Tesco where she spent to her heart's content on a stroller (called a pram) and a crib (called a cot) and diapers (called nappies) and all sorts of darling outfits for her beloved Emmy. She stocked the kitchen with plenty of food and even prepared two of her favorite casseroles. The freezer in Stewart's tiny English fridge was only big enough to freeze one of the casseroles, so she stopped there. Still, even one frozen casserole would free them up to care for the baby and work on clearing the house. Peg and Patricia had met at the hospital and hit it off immediately, so Peg volunteered to come and help with the clearing and packing. She also recommended a house agent (what Patricia called a real estate agent) to help with the sale of the house.

Odile's animosity toward her mother stemmed from Odile's control needs conflicting with her mother's. When Odile was a girl, she would ask Patricia to come help her choose her clothes for the school day.

"How about the plaid skirt and the blue sweater?"

"No, I don't want to wear a sweater; it's too hot."

"Or the flowered dress and your new sandals."

"No, I hate that dress. I can't play in it."

This would go on for several minutes until Patricia left in a huff, saying, "Choose your own outfit. I don't care what you wear." The same scenario would be repeated a few days later. As Odile grew, the bouts changed focus:

"Which college should I go to?"

"Your dad and I think you should do two years at junior college then transfer."

"Mom, only dumb kids go to junior college. Are you saying I'm dumb?"

And later:

"Should I buy the used Honda or the new VW?"

"I really think you should go for the used car so you won't have a car payment."

"But Mom, the VW is so cute, and it's my favorite color."

Eventually, Patricia stopped talking to Odile, except on reasonably safe subjects. This tense silence convinced Odile that her mother didn't love her. Mike stayed out of it, so

Odile thought the same about him. Her parents returned the sentiment.

However, both Odile and her mother had prayed and grown over the past year. Patricia actually went to a retreat house run by Benedictine monks in the Mojave Desert for a week-long silent retreat. She was keeping a journal and attending church. She volunteered every week at the food bank run by the Salvation Army. If their relationship was going to go back to their usual bickering, living together in one house, caring for a newborn, and packing the house for a move would surely trigger it. Both women prayed for help in the face of their coming challenges.

The day she came home from the hospital with the baby, Odile drove and Patricia held Emmy. Her mother started to object, but stopped herself---Odile was well-healed after a week's recovery, and she knew how to drive on the left better than Patricia, so Patricia backed off. At the house, Odile went up to see the nursery her mom had prepared. She had moved the full-sized bed over to one side and turned the other half of the room into the baby's room, with crib, changing table, and rocking chair. The baby clothes lay neatly folded in the dresser Stewart's folks had left.

As Odile put the baby down in the crib to sleep, she said, "Thank you so much, Mom. This looks very sweet and convenient. I can't thank you enough."

"It was a joy for me to do. I didn't want to over-do it, though, since we have to move home."

"Do you think we should ship this baby furniture home, or just buy new?" That kind of question had led to conflict in their recent past. Odile tended to say 'no' to whatever Patricia suggested.

"We can make some inquiries about shipping costs. Let's sleep and pray on it."

"Yes, good idea."

To their glad surprise, the two women fell into a comfortable and peaceful sharing of duties. Odile took care of the baby, and Patricia took care of the house. When the house agent needed questions answered, Odile came to the fore. She let her mother decide about what to keep and what to let go. She decided to let most of it go and called an auctioneer to come and look at the house contents. He said he would take the few good pieces in his van and auction them at his establishment, taking a percentage. He suggested calling Oxfam to pick up the rest. Patricia started to say, 'Well, at home we would have a garage sale' but stopped herself. What good would making such comparisons do?

She also stopped herself from advising Odile on baby care. She remembered her own mother shaming her for not bundling Odile warm enough when they went out. Her mother had grown up in North Dakota where babies sometimes froze to death; she did not understand California. Patricia decided she would let Odile do it her way. She knew babies were not as fragile as some people supposed. She intended to nurture her relationship with her daughter and granddaughter, now that she saw them as her greatest joy. Patience and humility had finally come to Patricia.

Before Stewart's house was on the market a month, an offer came in from a young family seeking their first home because a baby was on the way. Odile accepted their offer, and the wheels began to turn for the move. The auctioneer sent a check for the items he sold, the buyers wanted to keep any furniture Odile was willing to leave, and they paid her a good price for Stewart's car, too. In the end, Odile shipped only a few boxes of family memorabilia, as they planned to buy new baby furniture when they got home. They took only the stroller on the trip to California, along with their own clothes and the baby's.

Peg and Naomi invited them to dinner on their last night. Bede also came to the bittersweet party. The sweetness came mostly from holding Emmy and cooing over her. Even Bede, the disguised softy, held the baby every chance he got.

The bitterness came from the cutting of heartstrings. God had blessed the friends with a deep love and concern for each other, and though that love would never die, it would be stretched five thousand miles. Not one of them was naive enough to think the distance would have no effect on their friendship. They would never be as close as they were at this moment, and some tears fell while others were held back.

Bede said, "I can't believe I am going to quote Sister Lucy, but here goes. She once said, 'Love always hurts, but it's worth it.' And I am grateful to all of you for showing me new faces of love. You have been a gift to me, and I will never forget you, though I will let you go."

Naomi added, "And I want to quote Odile, who always says---"

"Thanks, God," the whole company said in a ragged unison. Laughter and embraces and farewells. Amen.

About this book and me, Pamella Bowen

I took my first trip to Britain in 1970 with my friend Kathie Kelly, right after we graduated from Pomona High School in Southern California. Much of this novel reflects the culture shock I experienced on that trip. I also attended a UCLA extension course at Trinity Hall, Cambridge for several weeks in the summer of 1980. When I wasn't studying Charles Dickens, I paid an undergraduate to punt me along the Cam, I walked the colleges, and I went to Evensong at one of the town churches.

My love of England has formed me in many ways, including attracting me to the Episcopal Church. Like Odile, I felt touched by God only when I crossed the Atlantic to the holy shores of Great Britain. When I got home, I looked for spiritual food in the American branch of the Anglican Communion. Also like Odile, I am a controller and egotist, working on myself via prayer and writing.

I have been writing since I retired from teaching high school English in 2009. I always wanted to write, but like most writers I had been taught that I couldn't. I had to make a living in a secure profession, they told me, so I did that for 33 years. Now, on my modest teacher pension, I have the freedom to write what I want and publish it. I started out writing country song lyrics, then Christian lyrics, poetry, children's books, devotionals, and novels. It's all been part of growing up and letting go of expectations, limits, control, and cravings.

I live happily in an empty nest with my husband Don. Our two daughters live in Nevada and Nebraska, leaving us here in Temecula, California.

Thanks for picking up this book. You have made my dream come true.

Pamella Bowen

Other Books by Pamella Bowen, available at amazon.com

For Grown-ups:

Magdalena's Demons

Labyrinth Wakening: A Spiritual Journey Novel

Destiny Fair

Bombs, Betty, and Bed-counts: A Memoir of WWII and Beyond

A Doubter's Devotional, 1&2

Play to God: Rediscover Childlike Joy

For Children:

Folding Memory: An Alzheimer's story

Faith and Grace Say Their Prayers

Faith and Grace: Puppy Love

Faith and Grace Go Birding (coming soon)

Old Vine and Little Branch

Pray for the World

Vid Viejo y Ramita